IN THE QUEEN'S DARK LIGHT

SUZI WIELAND

Twisted Path Press

Published by Twisted Path Press
Editing by Karen Sanders
Cover by Krafigs Design
First edition June 2020, Second edition May 2022, Third edition July 2024

Chapter One

The bright sun streams into the window of Starr's bedroom, and she watches two bluebirds chase through the trees outside. A carriage rumbles by on the dirt road beneath her window, sending up a bunch of dust in the air. They desperately need rain to dampen the dry earth.

In one more minute Melinda will be done with Starr's hair, and she must go downstairs to join the queen for breakfast. But as with any meal, Starr would rather not.

A permanent ache rests in her heart for her father, who died two years ago. His kingdom was strong once, but now Queen Ivy is driving it into the ground, taking advantage of her people and others. Starr has never been particularly fond of the woman, but her father's death changed the queen into something unrecognizable, someone who cares not for others' feelings, someone with an unquenchable thirst for power.

"I'm done." Melinda hands Starr a mirror and steps back so Starr can view her long black hair.

She ambles to her dressing table and holds the mirror up to admire her maid's handiwork. Two smaller braids weave around the back and join with a larger braid at the nape of her neck. "It's perfect, Melinda. Thank you." She glances at the clock on the wall. Exactly eight. "I suppose I'd better get down to breakfast."

"Your room will be clean, and your bags will be ready once you return, m'lady."

Starr scans her room: the unmade bed, her dressing table in disarray, and the pile of books on the floor from last night when she couldn't figure out what to read next.

"Thank you." Starr must put her things away at night so Melinda doesn't have to do it in the morning. Melinda has enough to do.

Starr sweeps out of the room. She doesn't want to accompany Queen Ivy on the four-hour train ride to Laddais, but Ivy didn't give her a choice.

Only the queen sits at the dining table, a maid behind her and the kitchen staff bringing out food. Too much to feed the two of them.

"You're late?" Ivy snipes. She sits like a stiff board in her silky red dress and that ridiculous crown. It's not the size of the one she wears for official functions, but still—the small headband encrusted with diamonds rests on her head to tell the world who she is, as if nobody knows she is the queen. Her blonde hair is coiled tightly in the braided bun she always wears, but her blue eyes glare at Starr.

"I'm sorry." Starr lowers her head and sits. It's only eight-oh-three. "Melinda was finishing my hair."

Oh no. She shouldn't have said that. Starr doesn't want the queen scolding her maid.

"Breakfast is at eight." Ivy holds her juice glass in front of her lips, her eyes narrowed in on Starr. "It is the duty of a princess to be on time."

"I know, I know. I'm sorry."

"That woman is too slow. We should find you another maid. Are your bags prepared?"

What? Melinda is a dream, so helpful and polite. "No. It was my fault. Halfway through doing my hair, I asked her to switch to a different style." The story is a lie, but she can't let Melinda get blamed. "And yes, my bags are ready."

A servant piles food on Starr's plate, and Ivy picks up her biscuit, poised to take a bite with her blood-red lips. "Next time, don't be late."

"It won't happen again." Starr doesn't know what her father saw in this woman. They met a year after her mother died, and Ivy and Father were so very different, but somehow he fell in love with her.

"Your Majesty." The steward steps into the room and waits for Queen Ivy to respond. "Lady Montgomery and her daughter have arrived."

"Send them in, Oliver. And place their bags into the carriage." Ivy gives Starr a pointed look. Hopefully Ivy won't send Oliver to get Starr's bags—they might not be ready for another fifteen minutes or so.

Ivy tells Abigail Montgomery and Liliana to sit after they greet her and curtsey. "Bring a plate out for our guests," Ivy commands a servant and smiles at the two ladies.

Liliana is sixteen, four years younger than Starr, and is usually quiet around the princess. Starr would try to engage her in conversation, but it'll be best to wait until they are on the train. Starr is pretty sure that Ivy intimidates Liliana, and that is why she keeps her mouth shut around her.

"You are looking stunning today." Abigail's eyes sweep over the queen. "Such a pretty dress. Is it new?"

"Of course it is. This is an important trip." Ivy huffs.

"Yes, it is, Your Majesty." Abigail pauses for a moment before pulling a paper out of her bag and sliding it over to Ivy. "I have a list for you."

Abigail is perhaps the closest thing to a best friend that Ivy has, but Starr wouldn't exactly use those words. Nobody is as high on the pedestal as Ivy.

"Finally. I told Oliver of the festivities, so he is working on it." Ivy peruses the list, her lips pursed.

"What festivities?" Starr asks.

Ivy gives her an annoyed look. "I am throwing a ball in a few weeks, and the night before will be a grand feast as well."

Now what? Ivy holds way too many extravagant affairs for Starr's tastes. So much food gets thrown away after these parties, despite the hundreds of guests she has attending them.

"What for?"

"For me." Ivy shakes her head like Starr has no sense.

Six months ago, the queen started on a journey to find a mate. Starr has seen so many good men visit the castle, but Ivy's expectations are very high. A prince from another kingdom has shown interest in her, but she only spoke to him for an hour before deciding he was too annoying. And she's dismissed others just as quickly.

"You should meet all of them," Abigail says, "but there are two especially that I think would be a proper match. Lord Emery, Duke of Hillshire, and the Duke of

Nawick, Lord Millane. I've heard Lord Emery is especially fetching."

"Well, it is a requirement." Ivy sighs. "I could not have an ugly king by my side."

A servant swishes by Starr and adds more food to Ivy's plate. She doesn't acknowledge it and keeps eating. Starr hates that the servants do that because she always ends up with half a plate full of food she does not finish, but Ivy's rule is to refill a plate when it gets half empty.

"Are there many eligible nobles in Laddais?" Abigail takes a small bite of food, like a proper woman. Starr stuffs a forkful into her mouth, hoping Ivy will see her and get annoyed, but Ivy isn't looking, too busy considering the trip they're about to take.

"There are a few I might consider. I was so disappointed with the Duke of Covington."

"And why's that?"

"He didn't see the value in the merging of our countries." Ivy scoffs. "But he is no longer a duke."

Starr lets out a laugh, and both ladies stare at her, so she covers it with a fake coughing fit. "Swallowed wrong," she says, and Ivy turns to Abigail. Starr busies herself with another bite of food even though she is full.

The so-called *merging* was more of an acquisition, by force, that joined the duke's kingdom, Laddais, with Starr's. Ivy had sent the delegation over to offer the merger, but they refused, and so she sent the royal forces to take control and oust the duke. Hundreds of years ago, that small kingdom had gotten rid of its king and royal family and had been fine. Now it's under the rule of a queen again, and many are unhappy about it.

Hence the trip so she could greet her new subjects.

The women talk a bit longer, and Ivy finally excuses Starr to retrieve her bags. Everything is packed as Melinda said it would be, and Starr gives her a quick thank you and grabs more things.

The carriage ride will only be twenty minutes, but the train ride will be four hours. Starr brings several books for their three-day trip and hopes Liliana will at least talk with her, or this will be a long and boring journey.

Starr stands in front of the main entrance to the castle, peering down the steps and over the green grass of the grounds. During Father's reign, townspeople were welcome on the castle grounds in front. The king would sometimes walk among those people and speak with them, bringing Starr with him. He would take time to hear their complaints, although more often they gushed over him.

That all ended once he died, and Ivy took over. She erected the guard house and very rarely allows townspeople on the grounds. Starr misses the days of walking among her people and getting to know them.

Ivy has control of the workings of the castle and kingdom and has changed so much. And unfortunately, this trip will be one filled with those rules of decorum and boring people who only want to impress Starr and the queen. She can't wait until it's done.

Chapter Two

Starr stares out the window as they leave the towering mountains behind. Father wasn't much of a traveler, and when he did, he didn't bring her along. The snow-capped mountains rise high into the clouds like they never end, and the trees seem to stretch on for miles as they descend the mountain pass of the range separating Reoli from Laddais.

An idyllic lake comes into view, and she can't wait to return home and share this all with her friend David. The lake probably holds some big fish, the perfect location for a day of fishing. Not that it would happen on this trip or any other trip she takes with Ivy.

Starr studies Ivy, who sits at the front of the car with Abigail. Ivy would be horrified to find out Starr sometimes sneaks off to fish with David because fishing is not a lady-like activity. But, also, David is one of the castle huntsmen, and according to Ivy, a princess must not associate with someone below her status.

Everybody in the castle knows Queen Ivy invites the older squires into her bed when she is lonely, but she will never admit that aloud, and if Ivy discovers Starr's friendship with David, she will receive a serious scolding.

Liliana gasps, and Starr turns to see what she's looking at. The sunlight sparkles off the water in the endless sea before them, a mystery to explore. Waves roll in and break across the shore in a way she never imagined. Access to the sea is a top reason Ivy wants the two countries to be one. That, and the mines in the mountains that produce precious metals. The mines in Starr's homeland don't have as big of a bounty as these.

"Isn't it magnificent?" Liliana says. "I've never seen the sea before."

"Neither have I. A trip in a boat or a swim would be nice." She has been told that the sea tastes salty and holds different creatures than their lakes and ponds at home. The women up front laugh, drawing Starr's attention. "But she probably won't let us go. This trip is not about fun, she told me."

"Well, at least I get to see it." Liliana slumps into her seat but pops up again a moment later. "Have you traveled to the Norwest Estate yet? Queen Ivy told my mother how heavenly it is."

"Norwest Estate?" Starr has no idea where that is. "What are you talking about?"

"The queen's new residence." Liliana gives her a strange look. "The old Nicoll residence on Lake Mead."

Starr glances over to the queen, who hasn't mentioned any new residence, and Liliana couldn't be referring to Eldric Nicoll's home. She knows quite well that the family would not move from their manor on the lake. They sold their home in town to take permanent residence there.

"Queen Ivy did not mention this to me." She can't hide the irritation in her voice. This isn't the first time she's heard information like this second-hand.

"Eldric Nicoll gave the queen their lake home. It will make a wonderful retreat for the summers. The house is large and the beach fantastic. Maybe the queen will invite Mother and me to stay sometime."

Starr is hung up on the word gave. Why would the Nicolls give their home to Ivy? She stands and strides over to the queen and waits for Ivy to look at her.

"Queen Ivy, what is this I heard about you acquiring the Nicoll residence?"

"Oh yes," Ivy gushes. "I have already visited once, and we shall have much fun there."

"We will," Abigail agrees. "Once you update it to your standards. Hanna Nicoll has the most dreadful taste."

"Eldric Nicoll gave it to you?" Starr asks, an uneasy prickle creeping up her neck.

Ivy huffs. "Yes, he gave it to me. I reminded him that we need to make sacrifices for the good of the kingdom. This home is in a strategic location and will be used for many state functions."

Sacrifices. Like all the bakeries, butcher shops, and others that were forced to lower their prices to what Ivy demanded. Like the mines that are now required to be open twenty-four hours a day. Even the servants at the castle who have to work twelve to fifteen-hour days, seven days a week. Everybody in her kingdom is making so-called sacrifices.

Everybody except Ivy.

"You stole it from them?" Starr sets her hands on her hips and glares at Ivy.

"I did not steal it," Ivy spits. "He gave it up willingly."

"And where are they living now?" The Nicolls have four children, and although Eldric is quite wealthy, could he afford a home comparable to the one they had?

"They will find another home somewhere, and if not, they can live with his brother."

Starr spins around and stalks to her seat. She has no doubt that Ivy has taken that house from the family and given them no recompense.

Ivy and Abigail return to their conversation as if nothing has happened, and Starr stews in her seat. Father did not act like the kingdom was his playground, and he did not over-work or underpay his servants. He treated the subjects well and did not believe they were *only* there to serve him.

Starr says nothing more to Liliana, and both keep their eyes glued to the windows as the train continues its journey. Pretty soon, it enters the outer edges of the town and begins to slow. Swarms of waiting crowds stand on the platform, and Starr wanders to the front again.

"What are all the people here for?" she asks. Are they waiting for another train? Ivy's private train won't be taking them anywhere.

"For their queen." Ivy gives Starr a look like she's a dunce. "They're excited to have a queen after all these years. They are curious and want to welcome me too." Ivy gazes out with a dreamy look at the crowd clustered outside in the heat.

People are cheering and clapping, and Starr doesn't know quite what to make of the scene. Nobody behaves like this at home.

Oliver marches into the car. "Your Majesty, we are ready for you."

Ivy stands. A maid runs over with Ivy's official crown and switches the smaller one out. She makes sure every hair is in place and holds a mirror out for Ivy to look at herself, and Ivy nods.

"You look absolutely stunning, Your Majesty." Abigail smiles fondly upon Ivy, and Starr rolls her eyes inwardly. The queen needs nobody to stroke her ego.

"Is everybody outside?" Ivy asks Oliver. "All the ladies and others?"

Several cars in the train are filled with maids and the queen's ladies, and men to escort those ladies, and so many other servants. Starr wonders if they are staying for a month rather than a few days.

"Everybody is ready for you." Oliver offers his arm, and she slips hers through his, and they parade to the doorway, Abigail scooting after them.

"What do I do?" Starr asks, but the only person left is Liliana, who will not have any answers. When Father was alive, she was always by his side when meeting new dignitaries or royalty, but not anymore.

Starr moves to the exit and stops in the doorway. The whole crowd is facing the other way, watching as Ivy marches to a stage escorted by a man Starr doesn't recognize. The gaggle of Ivy's ladies follow behind but stop next to the edge of the stage and gaze at their queen. Ivy appears to be the perfect queen: pretty, intelligent, and poised.

Instead of stepping down from the train car after Liliana, Starr remains, studying the crowd. Most of the people closest to her wear ratty and worn clothing with the area in front of the stage reserved for the better-dressed subjects.

The crowd begins to quiet, and the man claps his hands together. "Welcome, everybody. I'd like to introduce you to your new queen. *Our* new queen. Queen Ivy." He steps back as she does her queenly wave to the adoring crowds with the biggest smile on her face. The noise level rises again and tapers off.

"Thank you," Ivy gushes. "Thank you so much for this wonderful welcome. For so long our kingdoms have been neighbors, but now we are one, united under my rule. I am so happy to be your queen, and I look forward to meeting all of you."

Starr almost laughs. Ivy would have no desire to meet the man a mere twenty feet away. He shuffles closer to the others in his worn shoes, running a dirty hand through his greasy hair.

Ivy continues on about how wonderful things will be, how their little kingdom can achieve greatness now that it is linked with Reoli. Starr drifts off, studying a small child holding onto his older sister's hand. Children. She isn't seeing many children here. Ivy probably banned them to keep them from ruining her speech.

Ivy drones on and on, the people cheering at the right moments, and finally, she steps back. The man makes a few more remarks and then escorts Ivy down the steps and away.

Oliver appears suddenly next to Liliana. "Princess Starr, please follow me to the carriage. We have much to do."

Starr sighs. These next few days will drag, and she's not looking forward to them.

Chapter Three

Starr was wrong. That day and the next is a whirlwind of activity, of parties and games and feasts. They don't get to visit the sea, but Starr is welcomed into the fold of the nobles of Laddais. Not that they have much of a choice, but they have been gracious.

The ball at Lord Wallace's has been so fun, and Starr spends the evening dancing and drinking wine and eating all sorts of delicious foods. Lord Wallace, the man who introduced Ivy at the train station, is to be the queen's top advisor in Laddais, and his daughter, Lottie, is an absolute dream, introducing Starr to the nobles her age.

Starr and a gaggle of other girls sit in the parlor, recounting the evening's activities, but Starr is in the corner, lost in her own thoughts. As enjoyable as the evening has been, she is ready to retire to her room to be alone and rest her aching feet. Melinda will be ready and waiting, and Starr wants to share the details of the ball with her. She always listens to Starr's stories and often shares her own.

A pang of regret hits Starr though. Melinda had to leave behind her children to accompany Starr on this trip. Starr would much prefer to stay at the castle when Ivy takes these mini-holidays. She hates for Melinda to have to be away from her family for days like that.

"I don't get why she's going." Poppy, a friend of Lottie's, lets out a deep sigh. "Why does she get to be one of the queen's ladies?"

Starr covers her yawn, having missed most of their conversation. Her eyes are droopy; she should go to her room.

"Because she has nothing left here." Lottie shrugs.

"Did you meet her, Starr?" Millie, another girl, asks.

"Meet who?" Starr has met so many people these last few days, and she can't remember everybody.

Poppy scoffs. "Probably not. She was hiding in the corner most of the time."

Starr smothers another yawn. She might not even stay up to talk to Melinda.

"My cousin. Bronwen," Lottie says. "She's going back with you to be your mother's lady."

Before Starr can answer that one, Ivy is not her mother, and two, she doesn't even remember a Bronwen, Poppy butts in.

"She was lurking around. Lavender dress, plain brown hair. She always thought she was something special but not anymore." Poppy exchanges a knowing glance with Millie, who smirks. If Starr wasn't so tired, she might ask what they mean, but she is so ready to go to sleep.

She stands. "I'm going to my room. I'll see you tomorrow."

A maid escorts Starr upstairs, and finally she's able to crawl into bed and shut her eyes. One more day of who knows what activities, and tomorrow evening, she will return home and sleep in her own bed.

Her night of sleep is fitful, but she drags herself up in the morning. After breakfast is a cricket match and a performance by a local acting troupe. Starr hasn't had a chance to ask Ivy when they are going, and now is the time. Ivy is resting in her room, and although Starr doesn't want to bother her, she wants to know when they'll be leaving.

"Come in," Ivy's annoyed voice yells, and a maid opens the door. "What is it?" Ivy narrows her eyes on Starr, and she about turns around. But she's already here.

"Are we leaving soon?" Melinda has already packed most of Starr's bags, but Starr has a few things she will get herself.

"We are not leaving until tomorrow morning. Today is their Day of Penance, and we shall begin at four." Ivy rests her head on the pillow.

Starr sighs. Ivy could have mentioned this before.

But wait. Ivy is presiding over it here? Starr's mouth almost drops off her face, but she shutters her reaction. She didn't think they had it here too.

"Okay, thanks. I'll be ready." Starr spins around and slips out the door. Every other week on Sunday, Ivy officiates the Day of Penance, the time when everyone in town is encouraged to attend the proceedings where judgments are handed down by the magistrate, but it's also the day that punishments are carried out, including whippings or the most extreme, death.

Attending the Day of Penance makes Starr's stomach turn. She has no desire to take part at home, and she doesn't want to here either, but Ivy will deny her request to skip it, just as she does at home.

The end of this day won't arrive soon enough.

The crowd seems to double as the time nears. Four o'clock, the same time the Day of Penance happens in Reoli. Ivy chatters away with Angus, her senior advisor, and Gentry Wallace, and an expectant buzz permeates the crowd, as if they are excited to see what will happen.

Kenrick, one of the leftover advisors from Starr's father, has a more dour expression on his face than the others. He is a decent man, much smarter than Angus, but Ivy chooses to ignore his advice so often.

Starr studies the unhappy faces and weary eyes similar to the crowds that gather at home, and she can't help but notice the gallows erected at the side of the stage.

Starr's father never took part in the Day of Penance, not actively at least. Executions were much rarer then, and he was not the one to hand down the sentence to end a prisoner's life. Ivy has jumped into that position so easily though, eventually calling herself Head Magistrate and Day of Penance Supervisor. She doesn't involve herself in minor cases, but she always does for the significant ones.

At four o'clock, Gentry Wallace takes the stage and introduces the magistrate. The man reads through names and judgments of those convicted, from petty thievery to more serious crimes, and then he invites Ivy to join him on the stage.

She strides up, a smile on her face like that first day here. "Thank you so much for joining us here on our first official Day of Penance."

First day? Did they not have the Day of Penance before now? Starr glances over at the maid standing closest to her to ask how sentences were handed down before, but now is not the time to question the girl.

Ivy gazes over the silent crowd, a heaviness suddenly thick in the air. "This day has a strong history. It is a time to bring our communities together, to show those who have wronged us that they will not get away with their crimes." She waves to someone unseen off the stage, and three hooded men are brought up. The first man is led to stand off to the side of Ivy.

"Marshall Wallace, you have committed a crime against your queen, a crime against your people, and you are hereby sentenced to death for treason."

The hangman removes the burlap hood, and a few gasps emanate from the crowd. Starr stares at the faintly familiar face. The dark brown hair and that long, thin nose.

Gentry Wallace.

He… No, Ivy said Marshall. But he looks like Gentry Wallace. Starr searches the crowd for Gentry Wallace or Lottie, but she doesn't see either.

"Marshall Wallace, do you wish to confess your sins and beg for forgiveness?" Ivy shakes her head like he's a child who stole an extra cookie.

"Never," he spits at her, his voice dark and angry.

Ivy glares at him and motions to the hangman. The man grabs Marshall's arms and leads him to the gallows, to the hanging rope. Marshall climbs upon a wooden box and sticks his head through the noose, which is already taut. Something about this is not right. Starr closes her eyes, her heart racing. Such cruelty is not necessary.

She tugs at her collar as the hangman gives a final look to Ivy, who nods. The hangman kicks the box away, and Marshall falls, his feet dangling above the stage. He claws at his neck as he gasps for air, and then his hands fall to his sides. His body twitches as he swings. He's not dead; she just knows it. A proper hanging should snap a man's neck, killing him immediately, but Marshall's neck did not break, and he's being choked to death.

Starr hardly listens as the next man is readied, as Ivy makes a similar speech, and she can't bear to watch as his life drains away just as slowly.

Chapter Four

Ivy stares at her reflection in the ornate silver-framed mirror above her dressing table. Her blonde hair is in a new style of braid encircling her head that Starr has not worn yet, and it will look even better when Ivy wears her official crown. Well, one of her official crowns. She has four with the exact same jewels in this style.

"Mirror, Mirror on the wall, who is the most beautiful woman of all?"

The mirror steams up and then clears, showing Echo's face framed by her burgundy hair. Ivy discovered her magical mirror years ago, back when Adrian was still alive, and since then, Echo has become a trusted advisor. Ivy never showed the mirror to Adrian back then because he would not have appreciated her use of magic. He also would not have approved of Echo's insight into the king's decisions, allowing Ivy to manipulate him when needed.

"You are the most divine woman of all. It is no question." Echo smiles at Ivy. "What can I do for you today?"

"I need information on Lord Emery of Hillshire. Can you find him?"

"Give me a few moments." Echo closes her eyes, a look of concentration on her face.

Ivy did not have time to question Echo about the men on Abigail's list before they left for Laddais. She had hoped that a proper suitor would be found among their new addition to her kingdom, but none of the men there were acceptable. Now that she is back, she can focus on what is important.

She waits, drumming her fingers on her dressing table. Unfortunately, Echo cannot see everything. She can't see the past or future, and she can only see snippets of things that are currently happening.

Echo had been so helpful when the time came to bring Laddais into the fold, and she was the one to reveal the betrayal by the Duke of Covington. Marshall Wallace deceived her and made her think he supported her, but all along, he was working against her, trying to keep her away from Laddais.

He didn't understand how important their lands are, how important it is for them to be a part of Reoli. The fool did everything to undermine her authority, but he was a fly buzzing at her head, and she swatted him and his associates down.

Ivy smiles. The people of Laddais now understand she will not tolerate any treasonous behavior. Such a waste—Marshall Wallace had been a strong and dapper man, but there are many more out there.

An image of an elegant man appears in the mirror. Lord Emery rides a horse across an open field, his long black hair blowing behind him in the wind. He slows to a stop and wipes a sheen of sweat off his forehead. The picture zooms in to show his stunning dark eyes. He is perhaps a few years younger than Ivy, and that makes him even more desirable. He will be moldable, unlike Adrian, who was ten years her senior and set in his ways.

"A marriage to Lord Emery would create a solid alliance." Echo's voice covers the sounds of Lord Emery's scene. "A duke in this region might have much influence over the King of Westray."

"I know, I know." She doesn't need Echo to remind her that her relationship with Westray's king has not been favorable of late. He does not approve of her decision to bring Laddais into her kingdom.

"And now show me Lord Millane of Nawick." Ivy waits for Echo to bring up the picture. The reason it's taken so long to find a suitable mate is because of Echo. Ivy might have made a mistake and married one of the previous men, except that Echo shows her things

Ivy does not know about. Men who pretend to be one thing but then behave another way once out of the queen's sight. Men who pretend to defer to her but then laugh about how they will take control once they marry.

Ivy will not be controlled by anyone.

A dapper brown-haired, brown-eyed man appears in the mirror. He kneels and speaks to a small child wearing rags, then stands and pats the boy on the head. Two servants scramble out of the carriage behind Lord Millane, carrying baskets of food and clothing for the child and his mother, who wait off to the side.

"Lord Millane would also be a powerful alliance, but you already have a strong tie with his king."

"Yes." Politics are so very important when you're the queen.

The duke does have good connections, but Ivy must do some research. She doesn't want a king whose heart is too weak. Queens and kings need to make important decisions sometimes and can't always worry about the people who are adversely affected.

"What else can I help you with, my queen?" Echo asks. Ivy has no idea where the mirror derives her magic from or where Echo is. Echo does not even know.

"Show me Abigail. I want to see if she was honest with me today." The mirror has been such a useful tool to see which of her subjects are loyal to her and which are not. And Abigail must be on her way home in the carriage with Liliana. They're sure to be discussing which men will be best for Ivy.

But they aren't.

Abigail stands outside the carriage, talking to her daughter and Starr. Ivy frowns at the young girl. As usual, Liliana has her hair done in the same style Starr had previously been wearing. It's annoying how the younger ones copy Starr's hair and clothes. Ivy is only thirty years old, ten older than Starr, but they treat Starr like she's the queen.

Their conversation is boring, and they don't discuss anything about the upcoming festivities or the invited men. Starr waves the footman over to help Abagail and her daughter into the carriage, and Ivy can't help but notice the way the footman's eyes gaze upon Starr's face and her ridiculously plain hair. The girl is oblivious to his desire. Oblivious to the special smile he saves for her.

Ivy slumps in her chair. Starr used to be a gangly, ugly girl with a freckled face that everybody pretended to love, but she's turned into a stunning young woman who often catches the gaze of many young men. Even though she's twenty, she's just a child and doesn't have the maturity and experience of Ivy. The girl doesn't deserve the attention of those imbecilic men who fawn over her. Ivy had to cut a couple of suitors off her list when she saw the way they looked at Starr.

Perhaps it is time to find Starr a husband too, to get the girl out of her hair.

But there are more pressing issues right now.

"I'd like to see the dungeon. I have a meeting with the warden shortly."

"Yes, my queen."

Echo shows her a view of the dungeon, slowly moving across the cells. Each fifteen-by-fifteen-foot cell has at least two people in it, some with three. A wastebasket sits in the corner, and small mats and blankets lie on the other side. She can see plenty of room for more mats.

"Warden Patel should not be complaining. He can fit several more people into each of those cells." She thinks to the written report Kenrick gave her, requesting additional housing for the prisoners. The money can be better spent on so many more things than useless prisoners.

"I agree. Is Warden Patel asking for another jail to be built?" Echo asks.

"We shall see. Perhaps an expansion. Spending money on another jail is not prudent at this point." Ivy watches the guard as he crosses the length of the cells to the end, where a prisoner is calling for help. He talks to the man through the bars and then steps back, shaking his head.

"That is all, Echo." Ivy throws the sheer black drape over the mirror. She doesn't know if anyone else can bring up Echo, but she doesn't want to chance Echo appearing if someone happens to be in the room.

Ivy calls for the maid waiting outside the door. The maid removes Ivy's slippers and laces her shoes and checks to make sure Ivy's crown is positioned right before Ivy goes to the study to wait for the warden.

Chapter Five

Ivy's patience for Kenrick and the warden is wearing thin. She sits in her study across from the old fogey and the chubby, balding man as they complain about everything. The jail food, the lack of space, not enough guards. She glances at Angus, her senior advisor, and he looks as irritated as she is.

Why did she keep Kenrick on as her judicial advisor? Just because he was one of Adrian's most trusted staff. That's why. But he's created nothing but headaches for Ivy since Adrian died. He doesn't like how she's taken over the Day of Penance. He complains about the jail and that her punishments are often too harsh and don't fit the crime. He doesn't understand that people need severe punishments to keep them from repeating their mistakes.

"I think one reason for this problem is all the convicts." Warden Patel lowers his gaze to Ivy's sleek mahogany desk. "All the new laws that have been created over the last year or so. The jails are too full."

He can't be serious. "My laws help create order."

Kenrick clears his throat and looks at her. "Yes, Your Majesty, but it's not the laws. It's the punishments. Maybe… um. For instance, the theft law."

She sighs. This again?

"You think it's okay to steal from your neighbor?" Ivy tightens her grip on the armrests of her chair. Thieves are the worst, and Ivy is often the victim of such thefts. Her subjects think they are entitled to her possessions.

Angus shakes his head in disgust. He, too, has been a victim of the petty thievery. She is so glad to have him by her side. Adrian's advisors did not work well with her, and she's dismissed many trying to find those who appreciate her vision.

"No, of course not. But we have multiple prisoners who are in jail for six months because they stole something small, like an article of clothing. A man who steals a pair of trousers is jailed for a year, just as a man who steals a horse."

"But will that man steal the trousers again?" Angus asks before Ivy has the chance.

"Well, no. Maybe." Warden Patel folds his hands and wiggles his fingers, thinking. "But a year for something small is a lot of time. Perhaps it can be a shorter sentence for minor offenses. A month maybe. Or community service."

Ivy sits back in her chair. "A month is ridiculous. They will not learn their lesson in a month. And community service will be a vacation for many of them. Getting out of doing their regular jobs. I think not."

"But we're running out of room, Your Majesty," Kenrick pleads with her. He sounds like those protestors who sometimes stand outside the jail to complain. Protestors who want her to release criminals into society.

"There is plenty of room. I saw it myself." Ivy huffs.

"You were down in the jails?" Warden Patel's brows lower. "My guards did not tell me."

Oh, he's got her so upset now that she messed up. She hasn't been in that foul jail for years. "I've seen it."

"I was there a few days ago," Angus says, which is probably a true statement, unlike Ivy's. "The queen and I discussed it before you arrived, and you can fit more prisoners in there. Each cell should hold up to six people."

"Six?" The warden doesn't hide his surprise.

"Yes, Warden Patel. Six," Ivy says. "And when all the jails have that many occupants, then you may return to me, and we'll talk about building a new jail. You are allowed to find another guard to help."

"But—" Kenrick starts.

"If there is a problem with my decision, then we can find a new warden more in line with my thoughts." Ivy folds her arms and stares the warden down.

"Six will be fine, my queen. You're right. We do have sufficient space." Warden Patel averts his gaze, his voice somber.

"Good. You may go now."

Kenrick and the warden shuffle out of the room with their inane despondent looks on their faces. They couldn't have actually expected she'd reduce the punishments? Crime has gone down since she's made these changes, and she refuses to go backwards. This kingdom is on its way to being a marvelous place to be again. All because of her.

"That man…" Angus's voice breaks into her reverie.

"Which one?" Ivy asks.

"You know how I feel about Kenrick. I've made my feelings clear."

"Yes, yes." Ivy nods. Angus feels the same way about Kenrick that she does. And she is now leaning closer to dismissing him.

"But I mean the warden. If things don't change, we should find someone new."

Ivy doesn't have anyone in mind, but Angus might if he's been thinking about it. Their system has actually been working well, now that Ivy is involved with the Day of Penance and the judgments.

When Adrian was king, he left the judgments to the magistrates, but now Ivy has taken over the duties of the chief magistrate, who hears only the most important cases. It's only one morning of one day each week, and she is proud to be making a difference, ridding the world of these dangerous men and women.

Angus chuckles. "I have an idea that will help cut down on the jail population."

"And what's that?"

"I think it's time to make protesting a traitorous offense."

"Hmmm. Protesting a royal offense. Interesting." Ivy stands and walks over to the window and watches a servant weeding the garden. The protests are one of the few areas where incidents have not gone down. Those barbarians, like Marshall Wallace, challenge her authority, her ability to rule her kingdom, and Angus is right. Those protestors are disloyal to her, which makes them traitors. And the only punishment for being a traitor and betraying the queen is death.

"The only problem is that you would have to preside over more executions. But if you don't want to officiate, then I can take over your duties." A gleeful look appears in Angus's eyes, but she will not pass off her burdens to him. This is her job, after all.

"No. I am the queen, and I must protect my kingdom from these murderers and rapists and traitors." She wants to make sure those heinous criminals get the punishment they deserve.

Ivy steps to her desk and sits. "I want you to write that protesting the queen, my proclamations, or our kingdom is now a royal offense. I want it posted in the town square and other places by the end of the week."

"I will get right on that, my queen." Angus stands and bows. "I will have it to you tomorrow for your review."

After Angus leaves, she slumps in her chair. This will create more work for her, which is one more reason she needs to find a husband. If he can take over the duties of running the castle, then she can concentrate on the kingdom.

Perhaps when she returns to her room, she can take another peek at Lord Emery and Lord Millane. The upcoming festivities where she'll get a chance to meet them won't be here soon enough.

Chapter Six

Three days home from Laddais, and Starr finally gets back to her normal routine. She hasn't had a chance yet to visit with David about the trip, but hopefully she can find him today. Later today, she will sneak off to the huntsmen shed to see if he is around and then visit her fishing pond.

First, she must attend breakfast with Ivy.

"Your Highness." Melinda pokes her head into the open bedroom door. "It is time to eat."

"Thank you." Starr finishes organizing her dressing table and leaves her room behind, Melinda following her down the hallway.

"You ungrateful twit," Ivy screeches. There's a thump from behind the wall, and Starr holds her hand to stop Melinda before they reach Ivy's open door. "I have given you a second chance, and this is how you treat me?"

There's more rustling and another thump. "Remake this bed," Ivy snarls. "And don't make this mistake again."

Starr has been on the receiving end of Ivy's irritation, and she hopes the maid can fix the bed; otherwise, Starr will suffer at breakfast. She puts a finger to her lips and quietly shushes Melinda, and then she slips by Ivy's door.

She doesn't have to wait long at the table, and breakfast goes smoother than Starr imagines, thanks to Ivy and Angus discussing plans for the next ball. Ivy delights in planning activities where she can shine.

Just before Starr is excused by Ivy, a young maid rushes into the dining room and stands behind Ivy's chair. Ivy purses her lips and sets down the glass she has been drinking from. Her face turns dark as she speaks to the maid.

"Where have you been?" she snaps.

"I had to finish your bed and clean the rest of the room." The maid shrinks away, her body seemingly drained of all energy. Her face looks familiar, but Starr can't recall the woman's name. She can't be much older than Starr though.

"That is unacceptable." Ivy drums her fingers loudly on the table. "You were needed here."

How ridiculous. Ivy hasn't asked a servant for anything during their meal.

"When I say to be here," Ivy growls, "then you get down here."

"Yes, Your Majesty. It won't happen again." The girl nods, her eyes sad.

"It better not. Now take my plate away." Ivy leans back in her chair, arms folded, and the maid reaches around her and picks up the full plate of food. The plate slips, and she clambers to get a better hold of it, but the food dumps down the front of Ivy's dress.

Ivy squeals and jumps to her feet, and Starr almost laughs.

"You little shrew. You did that on purpose." The eggs and syrup-drowned pancakes drip down Ivy's dress to the floor, and she smacks the girl.

The maid cradles her red cheek. "I didn't—"

"Don't lie to me," Ivy screams and shoves the girl back. She stumbles and uprights herself, and Ivy takes a controlled breath. "Do you know how expensive this dress is? You will be responsible for cleaning it, and if you cannot get the stain out, then you will pay for your mistake."

It's eggs and pancakes, Starr wants to say, but she won't insert herself into the middle of this. The poor maid was just doing her job; it wasn't on purpose.

Ivy lectures the cowering girl longer until she finally stomps out of the room. At the doorway, she spins around, her jaw clenched. "Are you coming? You need to find me a new dress and clean this one." Then she stalks away, the girl following.

Angus stands, a smirk on his face, and excuses himself. He also leaves, and now Starr is by herself with the servants.

"That was a bit harsh," Starr whispers to Melinda. She trusts her maid, but she doesn't want the others reporting her comments to Ivy.

"Yes. The girl has had a rough week. First her father, and now this."

Starr's head jerks up, the puzzle pieces connecting. "What do you mean?"

"Poor Bronwen *lost* her father, and she's now working for the woman who took him away."

Bronwen.

Starr gasps. Lottie's cousin… Marshall's daughter. She isn't here to be Ivy's lady; Ivy brought her here to punish her for her father's betrayal.

Starr is seeing this vicious and dark side of Ivy more often, and it sometimes scares her.

Starr holds the fishing pole in her hand as David accompanies her down the path to the pond. Her mind is still rolling with all the new information, and she's not sure where to start.

He walks beside her, not saying a word, somehow knowing she is trying to work things out. The man has been like a brother to her, and although he knows of some of the queen's misdeeds, Starr doesn't know if he understands the depths of Ivy's depravity.

Ivy took away Bronwen's father, and Starr can't get the image of the choking man out of her mind. When criminals are hanged at home, they stepped off the end of the stage, which sits high above the ground. The force of the fall breaks their necks instantly. The gallows at Laddais were not at the edge of the stage, but in the middle. When Marshall stepped off the box, he didn't fall far. If they would have dropped him from a taller height, then his neck would have snapped, but instead, he was slowly strangled, feeling the pain.

They didn't just punish him with death, but they tortured him.

She had fought to push it out of her mind when it happened, but now she fully considers it. Marshall Wallace was a father to a girl about her own age, quite possibly a father to others. A husband, an uncle. Starr's chest tightens—a family lost the man they loved and depended on, and she's not sure what he did to deserve the punishment.

They reach the clearing, and Starr cruises to the boulders. The water is shallow but quickly drops down, the perfect place to sit and fish.

Starr dangles her feet, rests the pole on her lap, and stares at the calm waters below her.

"Too many things on your mind?" David asks, raising his brows so they're covered by his dark bangs. He's a bright and fetching young man, and she dreads the day when he finds a woman to spend his life with, one that will not appreciate him spending time alone with the princess. Maybe that woman will be understanding and will know David is like a brother to her.

She can only hope.

"Laddais lies on the edge of the sea, and it's massive and amazing, but we didn't get to go out there. And the train drove by this lake you would've loved. You'd love the whole area, the mountains and streams. Perhaps there are other animals in the forest we don't have here."

He smiles. "I have heard of the bighorn sheep. They have horns that curve like this." He holds his hands behind his head and makes a half circle. "And someday I will get to the mountains to hunt bear."

Starr shivers, thinking of the large creatures that seem so mean. Ivy sometimes reminds her of a bear.

"So you saw many interesting things?" he asks.

Starr pokes her foot out from underneath her skirts. Her shoes will need scrubbing when she returns, but if Melinda cannot get them perfectly clean, Starr will not punish her.

Unlike Ivy.

"Have you heard about Marshall Wallace, the Duke... I mean, former Duke of Covington?"

"I hadn't. Not until the other servants returned with stories from Laddais."

"I watched him die. I stood there as he took his last breaths, and I didn't want to be there, but I didn't really see him as a him. I knew nothing of him or what he'd done." Just like the other deaths she witnesses on the Days of Penance. Starr grips the fishing rod, swaying her feet back and forth. They hit the boulder she's sitting on, but she keeps bouncing them off. Sometimes it's easier to not see them as people.

"Marshall Wallace was hanged for treason. What he did, I don't know exactly. And I stood there and watched it, and I didn't think about his family, his wife or children, or anyone else who loved him." A tear slides down her cheek. "I'm sure somebody is missing him today." His daughter Bronwen, for one. Even the worst of criminals are loved by somebody.

"He has a wife and four children that are left behind, and he was planning an uprising to fight against the queen's forces. His brother betrayed him." David's voice is as somber as his face.

"Gentry Wallace?" Starr asks, and David nods. "He's Ivy's new advisor in Laddais, and Lottie was trying to be my new best friend." Does Lottie know what her father did? That he is the cause of her uncle's death? Even if she does, even if she disapproves, she could never say. "And now, Bronwen, his daughter. She is our maid."

David nudges Starr's foot with his. "It's not your fault."

More tears spill out of her eyes. If only Father was still alive, none of this would've happened. Bronwen would still be the daughter of the Duke of Covington, and Laddais would be under its own people's rule.

"I don't know what to do," she chokes out.

David offers her a handkerchief, and she wipes her eyes dry. He stares at her before speaking. "Things would be different if you were the queen, but you are not."

Ivy has many years left on the throne, and if she re-marries, the king would take over after her death, not Starr.

"You should have seen Bronwen. Ivy treated her horridly." The poor girl has lost her father and is separated from the rest of her family.

An idea sparks in Starr's head. She can do one little thing that will make a difference. She discusses the idea with David, and he approves, and after talking a bit more, they finally get around to fishing.

Neither of them catches anything, but Starr doesn't care. All she has on her mind now is rescuing Bronwen from Ivy.

Chapter Seven

"Mirror, Mirror on the wall, who is the most benevolent woman of all?" Ivy stares into the mirror, waiting for Echo to reappear. The gas lamps on either side of her table do not give off enough light, but she is going to bed soon.

"You, my queen," Echo says before the image is clear. "Nobody is as compassionate and generous as you."

"I am." Ivy pats her head and readjusts her crown. She's wearing her dressing gown, but she doesn't usually take off the crown until she's ready for bed. She wants to speak to Echo first.

"Your Majesty?" a weary voice calls through the door. "May I use the washroom?"

Again? That dolt wants to go all the time. Ivy glances at the clock. It's only been four hours.

"After you help me into bed," Ivy yells. The girl has been mopey since they brought her back from Laddais. She should be grateful she gets to work in such an elegant home like the castle, and Ivy is getting tired of the attitude. Her father was a traitor, and she should waste no tears on him.

"Echo, I want to see the home of Gentry Wallace." The man turned in his brother, and Ivy doesn't doubt his allegiance to her throne, but it's prudent to check on him. And evenings are the best time. After a long day, a man will share his secrets with his spouse as they lie in bed.

Echo brings up the image of the duke and duchess in their room, but their talk is fairly boring, until the duchess says something about their daughter.

"She's asking more questions about Bronwen, wondering when she will hear from her." The wife frowns at her husband. "We should have told Lottie the truth."

The duke snorts. "No. She was already upset about Marshall being put to death. It's better for her to think that Bronwen is living a life of luxury. In a few weeks, I will find someone to write letters to Lottie from Bronwen. She will have no worries after that."

"You are an amazing father." The duchess kisses her husband and leans into her pillow. "I never thought we could be so fortunate."

The duke pats her on the shoulder. "I know you worry, but I made the right decision. Queen Ivy will take care of us, and we will take care of her."

Ivy grins. Gentry Wallace is a good man, and she will reward him highly. Her biggest concern now is traitors. She's flushed out a few, but there is more. But who?

Kenrick? She hasn't found any evidence that he is betraying her, but she wouldn't doubt if he is. It might be simpler to just get rid of him so she has no worries. But the problem is that Kenrick was important to Adrian. He is loved and respected by many, including Starr, and she might put up a big fuss if Ivy dismisses him for no reason. Starr doesn't understand how tiring it is to constantly have your aides argue and fight on every issue. Kenrick, especially, doesn't see her vision for their kingdom and often tries to block her at every turn.

"Echo, show me Kenrick," she directs.

"Yes, my queen."

Ivy waits, but Echo's face wrinkles up. She waits another few seconds.

"Echo," Ivy snaps.

"I'm trying." Her face strains again, and she lifts glum eyes to the queen. "I'm sorry. I cannot see anything."

Ivy's lips pinch together. Echo is useless sometimes, unable to see the images Ivy requires.

"Do you think he's found some kind of protective spell to cover his tracks?" Has Kenrick found out about Echo? Perhaps he's organizing others right now to challenge her authority. Or he may be behind the protestors that are popping up more and more. Ivy grips the silver hand mirror Adrian presented her early in their courtship.

"I don't know," Echo says in a quiet voice, avoiding Ivy's harsh gaze.

Ivy flings the mirror to the side, it smashes into the wall, and glass tinkles to the floor.

"Well, you should know," she growls. "You should be able to see what's happening when I ask." Perhaps Echo is in on it too; perhaps she is a traitor. She sometimes does not see what Ivy requests. And Echo claims she can't see anything when Ivy replaces the drape over her. It is infuriating.

No, that can't be. She has provided too much information for Ivy already.

"I'm sorry."

"I want you to try again when you leave. You need to watch Kenrick and tell me if he is up to anything." Ivy does not have hours each day to spy on her subjects, and she must rely on Echo's help.

"Yes, my queen."

Ivy covers the mirror and goes to the door. Bronwen waits outside.

"Come rub my shoulders and tuck me into bed," Ivy snaps. "Then you may use the washroom."

Bronwen is not the best at providing relief for Ivy's strained muscles, but she will do for tonight. A squire is the best medicine, but Ivy doesn't want to go through all the work to get one up to her room right now.

"Yes, Your Majesty." Bronwen says the words in the most unappreciative voice.

"You ungrateful twit. Would you like to stay in my room instead and wait until I fall asleep?" Ivy huffs.

"No. I'm sorry." The girl hangs her head. She probably once had the ability to attract the side glances of men, but now her hair is scraggly and her skin sallow, dark circles under her eyes. She shuffles into the room as Ivy marches for her bed.

"Pick up your feet," Ivy growls. The girl better not scuff her floor. Ivy spots the shattered mirror again. "Oh, and clean the mirror up."

Bronwen just stands there, looking between the mirror and the bed.

"What's wrong?" Ivy is just too tired of this girl.

"What would you like me to do first?" she wrings her hands, and Ivy sighs.

"The mess, of course." She spins around and goes to her bed. "After you finish here, and after you use the washroom, you are to sweep the kitchen and dining room. You are to be up at five to start your chores. Do you hear me?"

"Yes, Your Majesty."

Ivy sits on the edge of the bed and waits. Finally, the mess is gone, and Ivy lets Bronwen dig at the tight muscles in her back. Then she removes her crown and lies down, and Bronwen tucks the blankets tight around her. Tomorrow has many tasks to tackle, and she needs a proper night's rest.

Chapter Eight

Ivy drums her fingers, waiting for Echo's pathetic excuses to spill from her mouth. It's been two days, and Echo still claims she can't see any visions unless Ivy is present. She obviously has not tried hard enough.

"I'm doing everything I can, but I'm not able to see Kenrick or anyone else while you are gone," Echo says.

"Worthless," Ivy barks. "You are completely worthless sometimes."

"I apologize, my queen. I don't understand what happens when you leave. It's like I just poof out of existence. I don't have thoughts unless I sense you here with—"

Ivy bangs her silver brush on the dressing table. "I don't want any more apologies. I want you to keep trying."

"I will." Echo gives her a curt nod. "I can see him right now though. It must have been a fluke the other day."

"Let me see him," Ivy huffs.

Echo brings up the image of Kenrick sitting at his desk, a pile of papers in front of him.

Someone knocks at the door. "Sir?" a man asks, and Kenrick motions him inside. Ivy doesn't know the man, but he is holding papers too. He stares down at them. "Am I reading this right?"

"And what is that?" Kenrick nods to the papers.

"The edict from the queen that sets all these new operating fees for the merchants."

"I'm afraid so." Kenrick's dour expression takes over, one she is familiar with. She wants to wipe it off his unseemly face.

"It's ludicrous. And the fines and jail time."

"It is not," Ivy spouts. The fees are a way to make sure all businesses are abiding by her rules. If the business misses two consecutive submissions, then they are fined double what they did not pay. And if they do not pay within six months, they will go to jail.

Kenrick grimaces even more. "It is the queen's way, and we must abide."

"Yes, you must," Ivy mutters. It is the best way to keep the markets running efficiently.

Kenrick stares at the man for a few seconds, and then he shuffles his papers. "Anything else?"

"No, sir." The other man turns around and leaves. Ivy must find out who he is, but at least Kenrick did not speak badly about her. She is so, so tired of this ingrate. At best, he refuses to support her properly, and at worst, he obstructs her at every turn.

She moves on to other sights she's been watching for the last few days. Lord Emery and Lord Millane. So far, both seem to be honorable men, and she wants to meet them in person.

Echo shows her a little of Lord Millane's activities.

"And do you want to see Lord Emery too?" Echo asks, and Ivy nods.

An image materializes on the dark mirror, and Ivy gasps. Lord Emery is in the tub, bathing, and she can't look away. He scrubs his broad shoulders and soaps his body. He is a stunning man, and she watches as he finishes his bath and stands, wrapping his towel around himself.

Ivy's body flushes with desire, and as soon as he is dressed, she throws the drape on her mirror and calls for her maid. Bronwen is off running errands, so another maid is waiting. She sends the woman to fetch her a squire to have a talk about *security*.

She has bedded him before, so he knows exactly what his duty is when he returns and finds her naked in bed. A good man knows how to please his queen, and he is a good man. He is on top of her when the door swings open. "I'm back, Your Majesty."

The guard stops just as Bronwen freezes. Her mouth drops open, and she gapes at the queen's naked body. "I'm... I'm sorry," she stutters. "You said to return at two." She shuffles backwards, gripping the sides of her dress.

The girl will tell everybody that Ivy is bedding a guard, a man beneath her. She will be the laughing stock of the castle, the butt of rumors and jokes.

"Do you not know how to knock?" Ivy yells, pushing the guard off her. "Did you not even consider that you should not invade my privacy?" Ivy jumps off the bed, stalks over to Bronwen, and slaps her. The girl cowers as Ivy gets in her face. "You are supposed to be the daughter of a duke, and yet you know nothing about proper etiquette. Your father betrayed me, and now you want to do the same. You think you can tell everyone what you saw, but you won't get away with it." Ivy points her finger in Bronwen's face. "I will not tolerate my staff spreading rumors and falsehoods about what I do in my private time."

"I won't—"

Ivy smacks Bronwen. This girl is full of insolence and shoddy work. "I am the queen here, and you will respect me."

She grabs Bronwen's hair and drags the half-stumbling girl to the doorway and throws her out.

Bronwen flails for a moment and falls into the wall across the hall, banging her head. She crumples to the floor, crying.

Again. The girl is a sniveling baby.

Ivy slams her door, causing her windows to shake.

The guard has slipped out the other door, which is probably a good thing, but Ivy needs someone to help her dress. She flings the door back open and looks out, ignoring the crying heap on the floor, and calls to another maid for help. She has things to do today, and she won't let this insolent brat get in her way.

Ivy has about had it with the princess's misdirected sympathies.

Starr glances over Ivy's shoulders for about the hundredth time at dinner, no doubt looking at the troublesome maid standing behind her. Bronwen's forehead has a big bruise from when she stumbled into the wall.

"What is it?" Ivy snaps at Starr.

Starr drops her gaze to her plate. "It's nothing. I just…" Her eyes flick to Bronwen once again. "I was in need of another maid, and I was hoping that I could take Bronwen off your hands."

"Are you kidding?" Ivy refuses to let this girl off the hook for her father's misdeeds. "No. I am training her how to be a proper maid. She has a lot to learn, as you can see."

Starr bites on her lip and frowns. "What happened to her forehead?"

At least Starr doesn't ask the girl herself. She has a bad habit of striking up personal relationships with those beneath her, and although Ivy has considered removing Melinda as Starr's lead maid for that exact reason, she will hold off so Starr doesn't push to have Bronwen.

Ivy can tolerate relationships of pleasure with the men beneath her, but not friendships.

"She tripped when she left my room earlier and hit the wall."

Starr twirls the wine glass in her hands for a moment. "Melinda would be a suitable teacher."

"I said no," Ivy barks. Starr always has a problem listening to her commands. "She is my maid, and I will teach her the proper respect she should show me. Her father apparently spoiled her too deeply, but he is gone now." Ivy turns and enjoys the pain that flashes across Bronwen's face. "Your life is here now, and you need to figure that out, or things will get bad for you."

Ivy studies Starr, knowing the girl is sympathetic towards the maid. Starr is as weak as her father was, and Reoli is lucky Adrian found Ivy all those years ago. The kingdom would be cracking apart if Starr was in charge.

"Don't you feel sorry for her. She and her family brought this on themselves. She is the lucky one, the one given a chance of a new life, and yet she is an ingrate. And if she can't handle her job, then she will face the consequences."

Ivy sighs. Why are there so many selfish and unappreciative people in her kingdom?

Sometimes it gets tiring.

Chapter Nine

"Your Highness, please come quick." Melinda pushes into Starr's bedroom and shuts the door. Starr rubs her eyes and blinks, checking the clock. Melinda grabs Starr's robe and tosses it to her.

"What's going on?" Starr yawns, stretching her arms. It's early… too early.

"Just please follow me, Princess." The urgency in Melinda's voice gets Starr moving, and she slides out of bed and into her robe and slippers. Starr rushes after Melinda into the hallway and to the top of the main staircase. A crowd of servants stands at the bottom looking up, a quiet murmur coming from the group, and Starr skids to a stop before she hits the first step.

A body hangs silent from the balcony above. A body dressed in a maid's uniform, with long brown hair and a bruise on her forehead. Starr grasps the railing of the curved stairs, holding tight as she takes each step one-by-one. By the time she reaches the bottom, everyone has gone still.

Starr stands in front of Bronwen and stares at the one slipper on the floor and then up at the body. Her head hangs so low, her chin touching her chest, the brown hair hiding her face.

The tears rise in Starr's eyes for the girl she did not know. Ivy brought her here, to be a servant after taking her father's life. Ivy probably beat Bronwen—she'd done it before to servants who disobeyed her. She punished Bronwen and broke her down until Bronwen couldn't face life anymore.

Ivy is evil.

Thunderous steps ring from the hall above. Ivy appears at the top steps and peers down at the unmoving body. Starr quickly wipes her wet cheeks, and Ivy stomps down the steps.

"How long has she been here?" Ivy growls.

"We just found her," someone says. "Shall we cut her down?"

"Not yet," Ivy spits.

"But, Your Majesty." Kenrick rushes up to her. "She is a young girl. Please, let us take her down so that she can get a proper burial. Think of her family."

"The traitors?" Ivy points to the dead girl's body. "You choose to fight me over this? Her family wanted to strip me of my power. They wanted me gone. I am tired of this, Kenrick. I am tired of all the battles I've had with you. You don't support me, and you never have." She narrows her eyes at him. "You are done here. I want you to leave, and I don't want to see you here again."

"But—" Starr barely gets one word out, and Ivy focuses the fury on her.

"Not you too. You are not above the law either, Princess Starr."

Starr backs away, holding her breath. Queen Ivy shouldn't be able to dismiss Starr like she has with Kenrick. Starr is a princess. But Ivy has just threatened to do so right here in front of everyone.

Starr isn't quite sure what the queen is capable of.

"I'm sorry, Your Majesty." Starr bites the inside of her lip, showing the proper deference.

Ivy spins around, facing the group of servants. "I want her left up here. This girl invaded our home and betrayed us all. She took her life and left you behind to do her work. She was a selfish brat who didn't deserve to live, and we are better off without her. So don't you forget it." Ivy marches to the steps, her lips pursed. "Now, I'm going to bed. Do not wake me unless it's something important."

Nobody moves until Ivy rounds the corner of the hallway upstairs, and then the servants' buzzing starts.

Bronwen is nothing to Ivy, a useless piece of furniture that broke and will soon be tossed away. Anybody and everybody is disposable in Ivy's world, and her darkness is spreading over the kingdom.

Starr isn't sure how much more of this she can take.

Bronwen's body still hangs from the balcony at midnight. Ivy has not mentioned her once all day long, but Starr can't sit there any longer and ignore it.

David stands below, holding on to Bronwen's legs. It's not like the body can be left up too much longer, but Ivy has given no orders to remove it. Starr will risk Ivy's wrath though. She'll tell Ivy she did it herself.

"Do you have her?" Starr asks, keeping her voice quiet. Ivy is in bed asleep, and no doubt someone in the castle will see them, but she doesn't care.

"I'm ready," David calls.

Starr leans over the balcony and lights the rope on fire. A saw would've taken her too long, and David needs to be the one to catch Bronwen so her body doesn't hit the floor. Smoke rises from the burning rope, the acrid smell filling Starr's nose. As soon as the rope breaks, David catches Bronwen and stamps out the ends of the singed rope. Starr lifts the end of her rope to stub it into the balcony, but the ends are not glowing.

She rushes downstairs to David and loosens the noose off Bronwen's neck, revealing an angry red welt.

"I'm so sorry," she whispers to the silent body. Ivy's anger at dinner yesterday, brought on by Starr's concern, might have been what pushed Bronwen over the edge.

The girl looks so tiny in David's arms as he cradles her, and Starr leads him out to a waiting wagon.

"Don't worry, Starr. She will be given a proper burial. We will take care of her." David's voice is thick with emotion, and Starr grasps the side of the wagon to steady herself, afraid her weak legs might give out at any moment.

She tries to hold back the tears, but it doesn't work. She might not be responsible, but Ivy is, and Starr doesn't know how she'll ever forgive her for this.

Chapter Ten

Ivy charges into Starr's room, followed by a maid holding some clothes. "Here are your dresses for this weekend's activities. You need to be on your best behavior to welcome Lord Emery and Lord Millane."

"Of course." Starr doesn't even look at the dresses and instead stares out the window, the sunny skies unable to cheer her cold heart. It's been almost a week since Bronwen died, and she can't help thinking about the poor girl.

"Starr," Ivy snaps. "Enough of this moping. I have been patient with you, but I am tired of this nonsense. That girl was nothing but trouble, and I don't understand why you are acting this way. *She* was part of her father's plot to overthrow my rule. She should have been on the gallows with him, but I saved her life and that of her other family members, and she repaid me how?" Ivy folds her arms over her chest. "With defiance and sass. She disrupted the affairs of this castle, and she is just where she should be."

Ivy doesn't even know what happened to the body. She never questioned anybody about where Bronwen went.

"Now," Ivy harrumphs. "You need to wipe that sour look off your face and be there to welcome our special guests at dinner. Do you understand?"

"Yes, ma'am." Starr nods, still avoiding Ivy's eyes.

"I want you to wear that yellow dress on Friday and the orange one at the ball." Ivy points to the two dresses and gives her a challenging look. "And fix your face. It's pale and depressing."

The dresses are horrid, and the only reason the queen wants her to wear them is so they will look dreadful on Starr. But Starr needs to pick her battles, and sometimes she thinks Ivy is looking for a fight. Not today though.

She pastes a phony smile on her face. "Those dresses will be perfect."

Ivy spins around and flounces out of the room, the maid scurrying after her. The door shuts quietly behind them.

"How much time do I have, Melinda?" Starr's head is heavy with shame over the recent events. "Do I have time to take a walk?"

Starr has been hiding in her room a lot since Bronwen died, and the sunlight will give her the energy to wear that fake smile. And Ivy obviously does not want Starr there when her guests arrive. Not a surprise.

"Yes, Your Highness. You have at least three hours before you must get ready. If you want to leave your hair how it is and just add flowers, you can have more time."

"Thank you."

Starr just wants to get out of the castle. David told her that Bronwen's body was placed in a field of wildflowers, but she doesn't know where. Maybe she will ask someday.

A warm hand touches Starr's shoulder and squeezes. "I will get food for you to take on a picnic. Would you like that?"

"Yes, thank you." A meal made with Melinda's love will make her feel better.

Melinda leaves, and Starr plucks a book off her shelf and prepares. She might as well wear one of her older dresses since she'll be taking a walk and sitting on the ground.

Tonight will be a stuffy dinner and tomorrow a ball, all for Ivy to decide if she's interested in either of the special guests she's invited, but Starr has nothing to celebrate.

Melinda drops off the picnic lunch, and Starr takes off. At the far corner, just inside the trees, she passes the huntsmen shed, where they clean and prepare the animals to be cooked in the kitchen. The men are probably busy inside.

"Starr, good afternoon." David sticks his head out of the window and waves. "Going for a stroll?"

"Yes. Some quiet time before the activities begin." If it were another day, she would invite him along, but she wants to be alone. Other than slipping out to see David once, she has spent the last week in her room by herself, or as much as Ivy would allow.

David gives her a knowing look. "Enjoy your walk."

He retreats into the window, and she continues. The sun shines down, but only shafts of light make it through the thick trees of the forest, and she takes in a deep breath of the pine scent. A bunny crosses the path ahead, and Starr stops for a moment to watch it, but it takes off into the trees, and she continues.

A small bit of stress melts away, only the birds and bugs accompanying her as she strolls to her favorite spot. The short walk takes her to a clearing with a pond, the water clear and quiet. Starr picks up a stone and tosses it into the water, creating ripples that spiral outward.

She spreads the thin blanket on the ground and pulls out her food. A turkey sandwich and fruit.

Whatever dressing was used on the sandwich is amazing. She would tell Ivy, but there's no point. Ivy does not eat simple things like sandwiches. That food is meant for the poor.

Tomorrow's ball will be better than tonight's dinner at least, and after Starr returns and dresses, she will probably hear another lecture from Ivy about her rules of decorum, none of which Starr would break anyway, and Ivy will add one more stern lecture if Starr still appears down.

Starr reclines on her blanket and lets the sun soak into her skin, trying to keep her mind clear of any thoughts.

A twig cracks behind her, and Starr looks up to see a man standing at the edge of the clearing. His long black hair is pinned at the nape of his neck, his broad chest covered by a blue silk tunic, and his legs are tree trunks, so thick and strong.

"Oh, good afternoon." Starr goes to stand, but he motions to stop.

"Please don't get up. I'll join you down there if you don't mind." He points to the blanket and awaits her answer.

His charming smile throws her off, making her mind mush for a moment.

She pats the ground, all thoughts of being alone swept away in the breeze. He takes a seat, and she remembers her manners.

"I'm afraid I have no food left to share." She waves at the empty basket.

"I am fine, thank you." He grins, his brown eyes sparkling. "You have…" He points and frowns, then grabs her napkin and wipes the corner of her mouth with it. "Just a bit of food." He tosses the napkin down.

Starr's face burns bright pink, and she hopes she has no food between her teeth.

"I'm Bard." He offers his hand, and she shakes it, then she pats her face once more. Ivy would chastise her for being such a dunce. "This is a lovely pond. Do you swim in it at all?" He gazes out on the still waters, and she takes in the site once again.

"It is. It's perfect for swimming." The perfect place to escape when Ivy becomes too smothering.

"I have a pond behind my home too. I have to share it with the frogs and fish, but they don't seem to mind when I join them."

Bard raises his brows at her, and she laughs. "I suppose I sometimes swim with them too, but they usually stay hidden here." She waves towards the tree. "There is, however, an eagle's nest up high, and sometimes when I'm swimming, I see him swoop through the sky. One time I watched it from under the trees, and he kept diving towards the water. I didn't know what he was doing until, on the last time, he flew away with a fish in his mouth." The way those elegant creatures glide through the air so smoothly amazes her. "It's silly, but sometimes I wonder if he'll think I'm a fish and dive at me."

Bard chuckles. "They have amazing sight, and he probably realizes that you are not food."

"I hope so." She laughs again, feeling a lightness for the first time after what's happened. "It's amazing though how they see a fish from that high and get it. I've sat with a line in the water for hours and not caught a thing."

A small smile graces his lips, and he stares off across the water. "It's been many years since I've fished."

"Well, you're missing out." Fishing is another thing Ivy would not approve of Starr doing. *Ladies don't put worms on a hook or filet fish.* "I could do without the cleaning part, but you can't eat it if you don't clean it."

Of course she is not the one to cook it. She is fully aware of how sad it is that she has so few practical skills. Her whole life she has been surrounded by people who do everything for her, and although she has no desire to learn to wash her clothing or clean her room, she would love to learn how to create delectable treats in the kitchen.

"The duties of being an adult." He sighs, rubbing his chin. He's young, twenty-five to thirty, but he must be with one of the dukes. "What are you reading?" he asks, grabbing her book. "*The White Devil*. Interesting reading for a lady."

"It was recommended by a friend." She snatches the book back. "I see you're familiar with Webster then?"

"Yes." He laughs. "It's nice to see a woman who reads widely."

Starr's face heats again. "So I assume you're here for dinner tonight."

"And a ball tomorrow." Bard nods. "Very important adult activities. I don't suppose we could skip out and come here to fish?"

Starr pretends to think about it. "A lovely idea, but as you say, duty calls. Perhaps on Sunday."

Her stomach sinks. Sunday is another Day of Penance, another hanging. The man sentenced to death purposefully burned the home of an enemy down, killing the wife and child, and Starr has no empathy for the killer, but she doesn't feel up to attending the hanging with the death of Bronwen so fresh in her mind.

"No, not Sunday. Perhaps Monday," she adds, the heaviness settling in her chest. Why did she bring that up?

"I will be leaving Sunday evening, but what is wrong with Sunday?" That grin is back on his lips, and she almost doesn't want to tell him the truth. Talk of executions will bring his mood down to hers, but she can't lie.

"A man was convicted of a horrific crime and will be put to death." The images of Bronwen's silent body, and her father's, flash through Starr's mind, and she looks away so he doesn't see the tears in her eyes. She tries hard to blink them away.

"Oh." Bard's face falls. "Why are you going?"

"The whole town is required to attend." *I am required to attend.* "I don't think I can take one more." A tear slides down her cheek, and she wipes it away. She's said too much to this man. Starr stands and shuffles to the edge of the water, not knowing if he will follow, and it gives her a moment to clear her head. She snags a rock and skips it across the pond.

She can feel his presence behind her, but he does not speak, and she can't allow the somber conversation to continue.

"Have you ever skipped a rock? I am the master, and I can teach you." She forces a smile on her face.

"Oh, I can skip rocks." He bends down and picks his own. He throws one, and it bounces one more time than hers did. "My brother taught me when I was young, and I quickly surpassed his skills."

"I guess I am not the master." Starr allows a small bit of happiness back in. She throws another rock and looks to him.

Bard stares at her for a few moments. Even though her eyes are no longer wet, she's sure they're red and puffy.

"It's been too long since I've done this too. I think when I return home, I will need to find time to do the things I once loved."

"You should," she agrees.

They each take several more turns skipping rocks, but she's never able to beat his distance or amount of skips.

A movement catches her eye. "Oh, look at that."

A squirrel chases a second one up a tree, running from branch to branch a safe distance away.

"Those guys are another reason why I like to come out here. Sometimes I'll just sit in the grass all still. They never come up to me or anything, but if I'm quiet, they'll dart a little closer to me."

"They are amusing." He studies the chasing squirrels for a few moments but returns his attention back to her.

"One time I'd fallen asleep here under the shade of the trees. And when I woke up and moved, a squirrel above chittered at me so. I think I made him angry."

"Squirrels can be temperamental." Bard laughs.

She loves the fluttery feeling inside when he gazes at her with his deep dark eyes.

They talk for a bit about the other wildlife around until he reaches in his pocket and pulls out his timepiece.

"I'm sorry, but I must get back to those dull adult activities. Duty calls, after all." He winks, and she laughs at him. "Thank you for sharing your pond with me."

"Any time." Maybe, once her official princess duties are over tonight, or even tomorrow, they will be able to talk again. Hopefully Lord Emery or Millane, whichever he belongs to, will not keep Bard busy this whole time.

"Good day, m'lady." Bard gives her one more wave before he strides into the trees. She then realizes that she never told him her name.

Chapter Eleven

Starr slumps in her chair after Melinda finishes her hair for the ball. She's feeling much better, but her body is still weak. She missed out on last night's dinner and most of today's activities because she was feeling ill, and hopefully Bard hasn't forgotten about her. She also crosses her fingers that he won't notice the circles under her eyes.

Ivy barges into the room, a scowl on her face. "You need to be down soon. The ball is about to start, and you said you would be there."

Starr would've skipped the ball too, but she wanted to see Bard before he left. Something in the sandwich she ate at the pond made her sick, along with several other servants who ate the same foods. Luckily it hadn't been too many, or Ivy would've been even more livid. She had been suspicious enough that Starr was faking, but Melinda gladly showed Ivy the vomit bucket next to the bed.

Starr quite enjoyed that moment when Ivy blanched.

"I'll be there." Starr sits higher and forces a smile on her face, and finally, Ivy leaves.

"Are you sure you're okay, Your Highness?" Melinda asks. She palms Starr's forehead and frowns.

"Yes, just tired. I haven't thrown up since very early morning. And that food you brought me was fine." About the only thing that kept her going was thinking about Bard. She should've asked him if he was with Lord Emery or Millane yesterday. Has he been wondering where she disappeared to?

"Let me help you with your dress." Melinda retrieves the gown from the bed, and they put it on. Starr looks in the mirror at the ghastly yellow dress. Ivy will love it.

A half hour later, Starr makes her way to the ballroom, her heart beating wildly. She will see Bard soon, and he will make her feel happy again. She enjoyed laughing with him yesterday.

A couple of girls her age stop her along the way, and she has to explain why she's wearing such an awful dress. Just once, she'd like to dress Ivy as horridly as Ivy does to her.

The music from the string quartet fills the darkened ballroom, and people mill around the entire space, talking or dancing. Starr finds her friends, and during their conversation, she scans the ballroom for

Bard, slowly sipping her wine. Thankfully her stomach is doing fine.

Ivy sweeps towards Starr's group with a man on her arm. Starr stops mid-drink. Bard is escorting Ivy, dressed in his finest. They stop right in front of her, and Bard gives her a wide smile.

"Lord Emery, I'd like you to meet Princess Starr." Ivy's voice cuts through the noise, and Starr goes pale.

Bard's mouth drops. "Princess Starr?"

Bard is Lord Emery. The comely man she was chatting up by the pond. The man she offered to take fishing.

"He's been waiting to meet you," Ivy says, no trace of that irritation she showed Starr earlier. "We've had such a wonderful day. You missed out."

Bard sticks his hand out. "It's uh… It's nice to meet you, Princess."

"You too." She shakes his warm, strong hand for a quick moment, and then drops it. The room closes in around Starr, and she can't breathe. She is attracted to the queen's suitor.

And he lied to her.

Well, he didn't. He never said he wasn't Lord Emery, but he never said who he was exactly. But she never said her name either. Still, what was the duke doing in the woods?

Ivy grips Bard's arm tightly, smiling coquettishly at whatever he's saying. Starr doesn't listen to them anymore, and soon Ivy is leading them off elsewhere. Starr stands there with her friends until, finally, a man her age invites her to dance. But then she sees Ivy and Bard there too, laughing and enjoying themselves. There are too many people between them, and luckily he doesn't see her.

But she wants him to see her so she can ask what's going on. He had flirtatious banter with her but is courting the queen. The questions build inside, but she doesn't get to talk to him.

She has to forget him.

But Ivy might marry him, and Starr will forever remember how she had once been attracted to him, had longed for his company.

No. It's not like she's in love with him. She just met him yesterday and spent the rest of the day thinking about him as she threw up in bed. But he made her laugh, and she so enjoyed his company.

The gentleman she is dancing with escorts her off the floor, and Bard steps in front of her.

"Princess, may I have this dance?" he asks.

She doesn't say a word, but the man she's holding onto releases her, and Bard takes her arm. She follows him out into the throng, and he pulls her close. He smells so good, and his eyes are smiling down on her, making her mushy inside, but then she catches a glimpse of Ivy in the corner.

"We shouldn't be dancing," she hisses.

"Why not? This is a ball, isn't it?" He motions to the people. "Would you rather sneak off to the fishing pond?"

An image of her kissing Bard under the moonlight next to the water pops into her head. But next comes Ivy screeching about Starr stealing Bard and ruining her life.

"Do you know why you're here?" Starr demands. Ivy will kill Starr if she sees their playful banter.

"I was invited to a ball by the queen, and you don't say no to the queen's invitation. But I'd much rather be elsewhere. With you, of course." He grins, melting some of her panic, and she shakes herself back to reality.

"No, that's not what I mean. Do you know why Ivy invited you?"

"Because I'm a devastatingly handsome duke." The sly look still remains on his face.

"Yes." Starr throws her hands in the air. "That's exactly why she invited you."

Bard stops, and they're the only unmoving couple in the crowd. "What do you mean?"

A few people give them odd looks, and Starr tugs on Bard's hand and leads him out of the room, checking to make sure Ivy is occupied. They sneak down the hall, to a quiet, and more importantly, private room, and she shuts the door behind them.

Starr's hands fling to her hips, and her desires clash: the longing to kiss him and the longing to admonish him.

"You didn't tell me who you were." The accusation comes out sharper than she'd intended.

"I did. I told you my name." He looks at her quizzically.

"But you didn't say you were the Duke of Hillshire."

"And did you announce you were the Princess Starr of Reoli?" His lips spread into a small smile, like this is a joke. "And typically a princess is there to greet her guests when they arrive. Not hiding off in the woods having a picnic."

The nerve of him. She would've been there if not for Ivy.

"I wasn't there because Ivy likes to be the center of attention. She doesn't want me there. Besides, I said I would be at the dinner and the ball. Before I got sick, I mean."

"Yes, yes. That is true. But I had no inkling that you were the princess. Besides, do you really expect me to suspect that the princess knows how to gut a fish? I was even surprised that the queen's lady knew how to do so, but I figured her father taught her at a young age."

"Yes… well… Father didn't teach me. I have a friend who is a huntsman, and he taught me. And what were you doing out there anyway?"

"I was delivering a gift of deer meat to the queen, and we brought it to the huntsmen shed so they can smoke it. Then I wandered down the path for a while."

He has an answer for everything, darn him.

"The point is that Ivy is searching for a king, and she is interested in you. Don't you see how she touches your arm and smiles at you?"

"Ahh." His face wrinkles up. "But I'm not interested in her."

"That doesn't matter. What matters is that she'll say I stole you from her."

Ivy fury will be taken out on many, not just Starr.

"You stole me away from her? I wasn't aware you had me at all, but I must admit I was hoping to see you again." He swishes a few stray dark wisps of hair off her face. "The radiant princess that I didn't know was a princess." Bard's fingers linger at her temples, and she can't tear her gaze away from his lips.

But this can't happen.

She pushes him away. "Ivy seems to want you, and—"

Bard kisses Starr, hauling her body close. Her knees go weak as the kiss goes on, until he finally pulls back. Starr's eyes stay closed as she takes in deep breaths of air, waiting for her heart to settle down. She's never felt such intensity in the lips of any man she's kissed.

She finds his eyes staring into hers, and his hand tightens around her waist. A sadness envelopes her. She hardly knows this man, but this connection with him is new and exciting. He was interested in her before he knew she was the princess, which means a lot.

But nothing will come of the kiss. It just can't.

"When we leave this room, we must act normal. I can't disappoint Ivy. I know you have no desire to court her, but I can't be the reason. In her eyes, I mean. And she will see it that way."

Bard sighs, long and hard. "I will agree to that, but we have not left the room yet. If you are going to pull yourself away from me before I even have you, then I deserve another kiss at least."

Starr wants to change her mind, to walk out to the ball and spend the night dancing in his arms, but she can't. This is how it must be.

"I can give you that," she says, the flutters starting back up inside her.

He leans down, and their lips meet once again, and Starr gets lost in his kiss.

Chapter Twelve

Queen Ivy stares into the mirror, trying to figure out what went wrong. She has already decided that Lord Millane is too stiff and boring for her taste, but Lord Emery is perfect for her—everybody tells her so, but he doesn't seem to respond to any of her attention.

She will give him one more chance, after talking to her mirror, of course, for advice. Their marriage would create a powerful alliance with the king in his lands, and the more she considers it, the more she knows he is the one she must wed.

"Mirror, Mirror on the wall, who is the most fascinating woman of all?"

A light flickers in the mirror, and Echo appears. "You are, my queen. Nobody compares to your wit and intellect." She pauses for a moment and continues. "What can I do for you today?"

"I am again interested in Lord Emery. I need to know some more of his interests so we can bond." The duke will be leaving sometime after lunch, but Ivy has until then.

Echo nods slowly. "I think I can help you with that. Give me a moment." She closes her eyes, and Ivy waits for her to get the vision.

Lord Emery is intelligent, so she will have to explain to him that she is the ruler of her kingdom, not him, but he will not put up a fight.

"I'm afraid I don't have good news for you, m'lady." The disgust in Echo's voice seeps out. "It seems the lord has made a connection with another already."

"What are you talking about?" Ivy's hands fly to her hips, and she stares into the mirror, whose image has not yet become fully clear. The bright picture slowly focuses, a scene from somewhere on the grounds. Ivy gasps.

Lord Emery is holdings Starr's hands as he stares into her eyes. That little trollop.

Her step-daughter.

Her Lord Emery!

"I told you yesterday this can't happen," Starr says. "I feel guilty already. We can't do this to Ivy."

Ivy scoffs at the ridiculous statement. Starr is putting on a show full of lies. She has no shame.

"Why don't you explain to her how we met at the pond?" Lord Emery kisses Starr's knuckles tenderly. "I did meet you before I met her, after all."

Ivy grits her teeth and clenches her fist, pacing back and forth in front of the mirror. They both lied to her face last night when she introduced Starr to him, and she realizes now that Starr probably wasn't sick.

She thinks to the night of the feast when Starr claimed to be sick in bed. Lord Emery had been around for dinner, but he left not long after that. He probably went to her room and spent the night with Starr. They probably laughed at Ivy, the poor widowed queen who can't find a husband.

The nerve of that girl. Ivy has given her everything, and she dares to steal Ivy's future husband? She's been trouble, nothing but trouble, since her father died. Before then as well. Adrian doted on the spoiled girl like she was the only thing in his world. Even after Ivy married him, things had not changed. Starr had a hold on her father that didn't disappear until he died, and Ivy had to put her foot down with the staff so they knew *she* was queen.

Not some ridiculous little twit.

This last week has shown exactly who Starr is, her sympathizing with the sniveling maid who committed treason. Starr's heart is too weak, and that weakness will only harm Ivy's kingdom, and now Starr has betrayed her, just like the others.

Ivy looks at the mirror in time to see the two kiss. A guttural sound escapes her throat, and she grabs her silver brush and hurls it into the wall.

"My queen, are you okay?" a tentative voice asks from the mirror.

"No, I am not okay." She thinks about many of the past balls, of the guests who were potential suitors. Many of them had danced with Starr, had even looked upon her with desirous eyes. Lord Emery is not the first. The girl has bewitched the men with her feminine wiles, and they lose interest in Ivy. That is the only legitimate reason that some of those previous men were not interested in her.

More memories rush through Ivy's head, starting with the time she and Adrian were married. Starr never wanted her around, was often defiant and belligerent. Adrian had said it was because her mother died, that she was having a hard time coping, but Ivy knows better. Starr has been unfaithful to the queen ever since she met Ivy, and Ivy won't stand for it anymore.

"I need to take care of this problem," Ivy growls, "once and for all so that this does not happen again."

Nobody gets away with betraying the queen. Not even the princess.

"What will you do?" Echo smirks at her knowingly.

"I really don't know. I need time to think." She puts the drape back over her mirror, unable to watch any more of this treachery.

First she needs to get through dinner with Lord Emery and then... The smile reappears on Ivy's face. Today is the Day of Penance, and getting rid of dangerous criminals always makes her feel better. It might spark an idea of what to do about Starr, because she can't let this betrayal go.

Chapter Thirteen

Starr stares at the fluffy white clouds floating lazily in the sky as she and Bard sit on the boulder above the water, her feet dangling. Her hand lies, gripped with his, on her thigh. She denied him by the water's edge, and he led her here, where she would have to deny him once again.

She cannot allow his kisses to persuade her.

"I understand that you don't want to upset Ivy, so perhaps we can do this differently," he tries.

"I just—"

He puts his finger to her lips to shush her and continues. "You can visit me in Westray. On official business of course."

"That won't solve anything. She'll be just as upset when I return home." This is all so hopeless. Starr has never wanted something so much in her life, but she can never have him after this.

"You did not let me finish. Perhaps you don't need to return home." His voice is tentative, without as much of the confidence it usually holds. "Perhaps you can make a new life in Westray."

Starr turns to his sincere eyes, knowing deep in her heart that he is an honorable man. A life with him would be secure and stable and full of love. But he wants her to leave her kingdom forever.

"What is keeping you here?" he asks softly.

Her mind struggles for one single good reason. She has few close friends, her father is gone, and she will most likely never be queen. There are not many she will miss deeply though.

"David," she says.

"Who's David?" Bard's words are laced with jealousy, and she can't help but smile.

"David is my friend. He is like a brother. He is the one who taught me to fish."

Bard's face relaxes. "And why have I not met this David?"

"Because he's a huntsman, and even our friendship is forbidden."

Bard tilts his head and smiles. "You seem to have a bad habit of forbidden relationships."

Starr kicks his foot lightly and laughs, but her mind darkens at the reality of this all. Sadly, she has very little keeping her here.

"I know what happened here just recently. Off Laddais and the girl Ivy brought back." Bard's voice has fallen serious again, and the emptiness claws at Starr's mind.

"I can't get the image out of my head."

Bronwen's gaunt figure swinging from the balcony. Starr doesn't know if the rest of her family was informed. She assumes David sent word somehow, but how are they dealing with it? The wife lost her husband and now her daughter. How many siblings did Bronwen leave behind?

"Ivy brought Bronwen here to punish her and made her life unbearable until Bronwen couldn't take it anymore." A lump grows in Starr's throat. "Bronwen was just an innocent girl."

Bard hands Starr an emerald green handkerchief embroidered with the initials BTE, and she wipes her tears away.

"I'm sorry," he says softly as he takes her hand in his.

Bronwen would be alive if not for Ivy, Marshall Wallace too. And so many others. And it's not just the men and women she's condemned to death, but those who she's hurt in other ways. Like the troublemakers at the mines. Nobody is allowed to speak against the queen, and now more and more people are being thrown into jail for exactly that reason.

Starr clenches her jaw as the anger burns inside her. Ivy is doing things that harm the very people she claims to want to help.

Bard shakes her grip off and laughs. "I think you have left permanent marks."

Starr glances at the nail indentations in his hand. "I'm sorry. I just… I… She's killing our kingdom, and I wish I could do something about it, but there's nothing I can do. The more I try convince her of something, the angrier she gets."

He takes Starr's hand in his again. "I understand. And that's why I want you to go with me." He pulls her hand to his lips and kisses her knuckles. "Come to Westray with me. You can be safe and happy and live freely."

Her life can only get better from here, but she hates to walk away from the only place she has called home. She is essentially giving up on her kingdom, her people, leaving them to fend for themselves against a tyrannical force. But what more can she do?

"I will," she says strongly, "on one condition."

"Anything."

"That I'm allowed to bring anyone with me. I want to offer to bring Melinda and her family. And David too. But that would include his sister and a few others if they want to join us. It might be a large group."

There are more she would love to bring, but she can't bring them all.

Bard laughs. "We have room for whoever you'd like to bring. We'll help them find homes and jobs and get them started."

Starr melts into his arms, the joy filling her once again. She can start a new life away from Ivy, away from the terrible things going on, and she will be happy once again.

Chapter Fourteen

Bard has been gone for five days, and Starr thinks about him often. His lands are six hours away by train, and she is counting the days until he will return to retrieve her. She wishes she could've left with him, but they did not have the time, and she needed to speak with Melinda and David. She could not force that decision on them and expect them to make it within hours.

Both have decided to move with her to Westray, to uproot their lives and make a new home somewhere else. And just as she told Bard, both are bringing their families, and she hopes it is the right decision for all of them.

Someone knocks on the door, and she opens it to find David. He's never spoken to her inside the castle, only when she finds him outside where Ivy is not watching.

"Good morning, Your Highness." He grins uneasily. "One of your lady friends has sent for you for a picnic in the woods."

"Who?"

"It's a surprise, Your Highness."

She peeks down the hallway, and although nobody is present, there are hidden ears all around. Maybe he needs to talk about their move. He, his family, and Melinda's have promised not to tell anyone so as not to alert Ivy. Starr does not want to deal with arguments and Ivy's fury any sooner than she must.

"I will. May I have fifteen minutes to get ready?"

"Yes, m'lady. I'll get the basket and wait at the back of the castle for you." His face sours, but he wipes it away, and Starr shuts the door so she can dress for an outing in the woods.

Instead of strolling down the path, David leads her to the stables and helps her up onto the horse. She wants to question him, but there are too many prying ears around.

They ride off into the woods at a fast gallop, the basket in Starr's arms.

"How is this spot?" Starr asks as he passes a small clearing. She's so glad he and his family are coming along. It will make her life easier having people she loves along with her. "We can talk safely here."

He glances behind them but doesn't slow. "Let's go in a little farther."

They continue, and twice more he says no when she suggests stopping. Finally, after an hour's ride, he helps her down. He stares off into the woods in all directions for a moment, as if looking for wild animals, and returns to her.

She unties the cape on her back to sit on, but he grabs her arm.

"Starr, please. You need to listen to me." He leads her over to a fallen tree trunk and sits them both down. The hairs on the back of her neck prickle.

"I don't know how to tell you this, but the queen ordered me to take you to the woods and kill you."

Starr bursts out laughing. How ridiculous.

But David does not laugh along.

"What are you talking about?" she asks. The forest seems to close in around her, the shadows growing, and the air becoming stale.

"Queen Ivy is furious with you over something. She wants me to bring you here and kill you. I told her I would, of course. You need to leave now and never return." His face remains serious, and his words sink in. "I can send word to Bard that I sent you in this direction, but you will have to find him yourself."

Ivy wants her dead? That makes no sense. Starr doesn't get in her way.

"Did she find out I'm leaving? She wouldn't kill me over that."

David clasps her hands between his. "I don't know what it is, but she directed me to kill you and said that when the deed is done, I can return for my payment."

"How much?" Starr is still having trouble processing this all. The queen has grown more vile and vicious over the years, but Starr has never imagined her to dispose of someone innocent.

But even as she thinks it, Starr knows that is untrue. Bronwen is one of the many.

"She did not talk about payment. Not exactly. She showed up at the huntsmen shed and sent the others away. Then she backed me into the corner and ran her hands between my legs." David's face burns bright red. "I think she would have bedded me right there if I had been willing." David swallows hard. "I'm so glad she spoke to me and not someone else."

Ivy wants Starr dead. She might be dead right now if Ivy had asked someone other than David.

"What am I supposed to do?" Starr chokes out, and another thought hits her. "Wait, she will kill you if you don't do the job."

"There is a path over yonder that you should take." He points behind them at a break in the trees. "There are houses along that way that do not back the queen.

They will help you. Tell them you are looking for the Queen's Rejects, and they will do whatever is necessary. If they don't know the name or if they behave unfavorably, then leave because they might be loyal to Ivy."

"Who are the Queen's Rejects?"

"They are…" He pauses and gives her a wistful look. "I don't know much about them, but I know that they are in opposition to the queen. They disagree with many of the dangerous and harmful changes she's made of late."

"Is Bard a part of them?" Had Ivy been ready to court a man who might want to overthrow her?

He shakes his head. "All I know is that he cares for you and was willing to help us. And he is the only one who I know will help you now." He grips her hands and squeezes. "So you must go now, Your Highness."

Starr doesn't want to leave him. "But what about you? Why don't you come with me?"

David cups her cheek. "Don't worry about me. I will bring back the blood of a rabbit, and the queen will believe you dead. But she will hunt us down if I don't return. You need to find someone with the Queen's Rejects who will help you find Bard, and once you find him, you can bring us to Westray with you."

Starr looks at her feet. He makes it sound so easy.

David grabs the picnic basket. "I have a change of clothes to make you look like a regular villager, and I have food and a waterskin and gold coins. That should help you." He stands, the worry shading his face. "I must go. I need to find a rabbit."

"Thank you." She has so much more she needs to say. David saved her life, and she isn't sure how to thank him properly.

"Someone will return for you as soon as you get word to Bard, but I am uncertain how long that will take."

"I will be fine." She says her words more confidently than she feels. But she doesn't want him to worry.

"I know you will." David leans in and kisses her on the forehead. "Be safe, Princess."

"You too." Her heart breaks, wishing so badly he would accompany her, but Ivy won't give up the search for them if she knows she's been betrayed.

He mounts the horse and gallops off down the path, leaving her behind in the silent, shadowy forest.

She's alone, and she should be dead.

Chapter Fifteen

Starr sits on the tree trunk for a long while, not knowing what to do. She twists and untwists the bottom of her skirt. First thing is to change her clothes. Not all the people around here will recognize her, but they will see the quality of her clothing and her hair.

She unwinds her fancy braided hair, wondering if she should rub dirt on her hands or face. No, that is probably unnecessary. She splits her black hair down the middle and does two side braids similar to the styles the commoners wear. Then she digs in the bag and changes her clothes to the scratchy brown skirt and dark shirt. He'd even included a pair of worn leatherettes instead of her shiny shoes.

She stares at her drab clothes. What would Bard think of her now? She supposes he prefers her being a fugitive on the run from the queen rather than see her dead. She desires the security of his arms and the warmth of his laugh, but she has neither right now.

Starr dresses and folds her former clothes and places them in her basket, along with her shoes. At least the commoner leatherettes are more suitable for long walks and hard work.

There isn't much she can do now but continue on and hope she finds someone who can help her get a message to Bard. She finds the path and walks for at least a half hour before she sees the first house, a quiet cottage with dark shingles. She knocks on the door and waits, pulling her cloak tighter.

"Greetings," a man says, peering out at her.

"Good afternoon," she replies. "I'm looking for the Queen's Rejects." She sucks in a hard breath. She shouldn't have said that right off the bat. Maybe the man knows what that means, and he'll turn her in to the queen.

"Who?" He adjusts his glasses and stares suspiciously, and she bows so he won't recognize her.

"Um, the Queen's Rejects."

"I have no idea what you mean. Who are the Queen's Rejects?" Just because he doesn't know the name doesn't mean he is loyal to the queen, but she can't chance it.

An idea forms. "It's the name of an actor's group performing in the area. You've never heard of them?" She wraps the end of her braid around her finger, hoping he'll believe her.

He shakes his head.

"Okay, thank you. I'll be on my way." She spins around and hurries down the path to the road, hoping for better luck.

She trudges to find the next home and the next home and the next, but nobody knows a thing.

The day slowly passes, and Starr's feet ache. All she wants is to close her eyes and rest, and for Bard to sweep in and steal her away. She spends most of her time dreaming of their new life in Westray. If only it'd been a few weeks later; she would be safe in Westray.

None of the people at any of the six homes she's stopped at have known anything about the Queen's Rejects. One man offers her a drink and a place to rest her weary legs, but she has a funny feeling and continues on her way.

Perhaps David is wrong, but she hopes not.

At the next house, she knocks on the door. This one has to be the right house.

A stern woman answers. "Yes?"

"Good day. I was wondering if you'd heard of the Queen's Rejects."

The woman gasps and sets her hand on her heart. "What would you want with that group of traitorous hooligans?"

Starr's stomach sinks. She has to fix this. She matches the woman's horrified face. "I wasn't looking for them. I was… was going around and informing people about their evil deeds." She hopes the woman won't question her about those exact deeds. "We need to let Queen Ivy know if something is going on with our neighbors."

The woman pats Starr on the arm. "Good, good. I haven't spotted anything unusual with any of my neighbors, but I'm watching. I will inform the sheriff if I see anything suspicious."

Now Starr wonders if the Sheriff is under Ivy's control too.

"Thank you, ma'am. We need more decent people like you." Starr spins around so the woman doesn't see the disgust on her face. Neighbors turning in neighbors. Ivy will probably string up anyone named as an associate of the Queen's Rejects. She probably has known about the group but hasn't mentioned their name.

Starr treks farther and crosses a small dirt path that leads off the main road. She peers into the trees but can't see a house back there. A second house lies down the road not too far away, the smoke rising from the brick chimney, and who knows how far into the woods this house is.

But she shouldn't pass any by without asking. David said they are out here. She's checked so many houses now, and this one is bound to be the one. She sighs and starts down the dirt path. The cottage finally appears, and she stops. Shingles are missing from the roof, and the shutters on the windows need major repair. And the crumbling steps. She doesn't want this house to be like the one with the creepy man and almost backs up, but she spots a pile of marbles sitting alongside a crudely made skipping rope.

Perhaps children live here with their loving parents. Parents who can take her in and provide safety. It is too much to ask for.

Starr strolls to the front steps and knocks on the door. A boy opens it and peers up at her with big brown eyes and little crumbles of food on his chin.

"Good day. May I speak with your parents, please?" She tries to look over his shoulder, but the door isn't open very wide.

The door slams, and Starr jumps back. That was strange. She almost walks away but decides to stay and wait. He might just be a nervous child.

Thirty seconds drag into a minute, and then two. Maybe he is home alone. But why did he answer the door then? Starr steps onto the grass, but the door opens.

An older boy with a pimply face stares out at her with suspicious eyes, clearly the brother of the little one.

He's not a child anymore, but not yet a young man. "Can I help you?" he asks.

"Could I please speak to your mother or father?"

"What about?" His voice is flat, and she can't read him. Children usually do not speak to their elders in such a way.

"That is something I need to discuss with them." She keeps her voice upbeat, but she's so tired of all this. Ivy wants her dead, and she just wants to find someone who can help her.

"They can't talk right now."

Although the door is open slightly, he's wedged his foot behind it so she cannot open it farther.

"I can wait."

"They're working. They're not home." He narrows his eyes at her. "What do you want?"

Who is this ridiculous child? "That's none of your business."

"You're on my front steps asking to speak to my parents. That is my business." His chest puffs up like he is proud of himself. The nerve of this boy.

She has been walking for hours, she is starving but hasn't wanted to eat her food because she doesn't know how long it'll need to last, she's run into a crazy woman who spies on her neighbors, and all of this is because Ivy wants her dead.

Starr flings her hands up, her voice strained. "Fine. I'll tell you. I'm looking for the Queen's Rejects so they can help me. And now, can you tell me if your parents know about them?" She slaps her hands on her hips. "Tell me then, Mr. Smarty."

The boy grimaces, blinking rapidly at her. "No. I don't know who the Queen's Rejects are."

The picnic basket slips off Starr's arm and falls to the step, spilling its contents. She will never find these people and get word to Bard. They probably don't exist.

Her eyes mist up, and she kneels down and tries to stuff everything into the basket. She grabs her cream shoe, now stained from the woods, and sniffs hard. She isn't a princess anymore, and her future is uncertain. She might even need to change her name to keep herself safe.

Starr is gone.

She picks up the waterskin, and the top falls off, water spilling everywhere. Most of the water is gone. What else could go wrong today?

She looks up. The door is now closed, and she takes in a sharp breath. What if the boy lied to her? What if he knows of the Queen's Rejects and is informing somebody who will cause her harm? They're making a plan right now, figuring out what to do with the girl looking for this traitorous group. Or maybe he's run off to tell the authorities. This is a mistake.

Starr needs to move on and do it now before someone returns and takes her back to the queen. She wipes her nose and stands, but the door opens again and stops her dead.

Chapter Sixteen

The pimply boy stares at Starr with wide eyes. "Do you need a drink?" He glances at the waterskin in her hand and holds up a half-full tin cup of water.

"Yes, thank you," she chokes out. Some tension drains from her body. He was getting her water, and she had thought he was about to cause her harm. She rolls her aching shoulders and reaches for the cup. She wants to climb into bed and get some rest, but she'll have to sleep in the woods among the trees.

He looks behind him and then to her, holding tight to the door. "Go around the back. The well is there, and you can have more water. I'll be out soon."

She nods, her head hanging, and trudges around the house. A fire pit sits in a clearing, a bunch of cut tree trunks surrounding it, and she takes a seat. She has no energy to even walk to the well and get more water. Night will be coming soon, and she has few options.

Someone clears their throat, and Starr looks up. The boy holds a stained and worn platter with a few pieces of bread.

"Thank you." She takes the bread, and he dumps water from a second cup into her empty one.

The boy sits on an adjacent log and watches her. "My um, parents, they won't be back until later. Maybe eight o'clock. You can wait here until then. They might let you stay in the shed if you need a place to sleep."

Starr lets out a snort. Princess to vagabond in a matter of hours. Nobody will recognize her now.

But at least she'll have a roof to sleep under. She glances up to the boy, her heart filling with gratitude. His parents might not let her stay, but he is the first person to help her.

"Thank you so much. That means a lot to me." She studies their small two-story house. "I mean it. I've been on my feet for a while."

The boy sticks out his hand. "I'm Garth. And that's Gaspar." He points to the chicken coop, and then the trees. "And Gary."

Starr does a double-take. Half-hiding behind the coop is a boy, and in the woods is the first one who answered the door. The boy by the trees, Gary, skips out, but the other one stays by the shed.

Gary plops down onto a log in his worn shirt and trousers. "What's your name?"

"I… I'm Starr." She sucks in a heavy breath. She shouldn't have said her name. "I mean… Stacey."

The young boy's nose wrinkles, his long bangs falling into his eyes. He swipes them away. "Is it Starr or Stacey?"

"Stacey." She nods. She should've been better prepared.

"I'm Gary. And I helped make your bread. Gaspar teased me because the loaf was all lumpy, but Garth said it tastes the same whether it's lumpy or not."

Starr shoots a look to the boy by the shed, but all she sees is a flash as he disappears completely.

"Your bread is fine." Garth smiles like a proud parent. "It was his first loaf."

"I'm six now." Gary holds up five fingers, and Starr hides her smile. "I'm allowed to use the oven."

Oh goodness. That's a little young. "And what does your mother say about that?"

Gary's face falls.

"She's proud of him," Garth says quickly. "It won't be long, and he'll be a proper baker as she was." He pats Gary on the back. "Get your skipping rope and show Stacey what you can do."

Gary's eyes light up. "Okay. Maybe Gaspar will too. He's better than me. But not by much." Gary laughs and runs off to the front.

In seconds, he rushes back and starts performing his *special* jumps, as he calls them. He can't entice

Gaspar out, but he doesn't seem to mind being on stage, singing as he skips.

Garth excuses himself and goes inside the house, but she sees his face watching her from the window. Gary entertains her with his songs and jumping, and even hands over the rope to her.

"I don't have your moves," Starr says. She swings the rope and jumps. It gets caught in her skirt, and she stops to untangle it. Skipping with a skirt isn't easy, and it's been years since she's done it. She tries a few more times, and Gary claps when she gets it.

"I think I'll leave the skipping to you." She hands the rope to Gary.

"That's a smart idea." He nods solemnly and begins to jump, and Starr takes a peek to see if Gaspar will show his face, but he remains hidden. All three boys are dressed in worn clothes, each having at least one or two holes in their trousers, but Garth's clothes are clean. Gary's, not so much, but she figures that is due to his playing in the yard.

"Gary, I need to use the washroom. Can you show me where it is, please?"

Gary laughs. "We only have an outhouse." He waves for her to follow to a shack off the side of the house. She stares at the wooden door that hangs open. She's never used an outhouse before. Of course she knows not all houses have indoor washrooms, but she's never been in one.

"The well is there if you want to wash your hands." Gary points to the pump handle by the house. "Giles yells at me if I don't wash my hands."

"Who is Giles?" she asks.

"My brother," he says nonchalantly. "He's working now."

Starr does a quick count in her head. Gary, Gaspar, Garth, and now Giles. So many Gs.

"Thank you." This is her life now, and she'll have to get used to outhouses and scratchy clothes and worn shoes and all that. Until Bard finds her, at least. She hopes that comes sooner than later.

She uses the stinky outhouse and hurries to the pump to wash her hands. At least they have water.

As soon as she returns to Gary, he sticks his hand out at her, a ladybug crawling on his palm. She laughs as he tells a story about it and then rambles on about the bugs in the yard. And the woods and the creek at the edge of their property.

"Gary," a gruff voice says.

Starr straightens and stares at the tall boy in front of her. Nowhere old enough to be Gary's father, but he isn't a kid either. His hair is lighter than Gary's, but he has the same brown eyes. Except they show a weariness and suspicion that a young Gary does not have.

Gary pops out of his seat. "Stacey, this is my big brother Gage." His nose scrunches up. "They're all my big brothers. I'm the youngest."

"I'm Stacey," Starr says, careful to not mess up her name again.

Gage nods at her. "You can come inside." He turns around, and she follows. His dusty boots clomp across the grass, dirty like his trousers and shirt.

Starr doesn't get the creepy feeling as she had with that man earlier, so she follows Gage inside.

Chapter Seventeen

Gage says nothing as he removes his boots and leaves them by a rug at the door, then points to a table. Perhaps he is the last one to test her before they bring out their parents.

Another boy sits there, one close to Gage's age. Starr glances at the clock, shocked to see it is almost eight-thirty. Where has the time gone?

Gage pulls out his chair and sits at the set table. Several bowls of stew wait, and she spots Garth by the stove. The door slams shut, and Gary runs into the room, Gaspar trailing him. Both boys hurry to the stove and dish up the stew. Gage scans the table and all the other boys quickly, and slides his bowl closer to him.

"I'm Garrick." The blond boy across from her nods. He's older than Garth and is showing signs of becoming a man. But he hasn't yet left his youth either. "Help yourself." He points to the bowl filled with little meat and few vegetables.

"Thank you." She pulls it towards her, her stomach ready for nourishment.

"So Garth says you're here about the Queen's Rejects," the oldest boy says, and she struggles to remember his name. Garrick, she thinks. No, Gage. Too many G names.

"Yes…" She shouldn't admit too much. She's already spouted off to Garth though that she's looking for help from them. "I'd like to talk to your parents."

"They're dead," Gage says, so matter-of-fact that Starr isn't sure she heard right.

"I'm sorry?"

"They're dead," Gage repeats. "Our mother died in an explosion in the mines, and when our father protested because of the unsafe working conditions, the queen had him thrown in jail where another prisoner beat him to death." Gage stares at her, anger heating his voice.

Starr scans each of the boys' faces. Garth stands in front of the stove, Gaspar and Gary on either side of him. Gage and Garrick practically glare at her from across the table, and she spies one more boy she hasn't seen yet. She does a quick count. Six boys. And no mother or father.

"Your parents are gone?" She blinks back the pain welling inside her of all the deaths lately. Hers almost being the most recent.

"Yes," Gage grunts.

She'd never wish losing a parent on anybody, and she'd give anything to see her parents again. "I lost mine too. My mom died a long time ago, but my father only two years ago."

"Why are you here?" Gage asks, tapping his spoon on the table. His eyes show that he's lived a lifetime at such a young age.

She's already revealed too much anyway, so she might as well finish.

"I need help. I was advised to find someone with the Queen's Rejects. That they could help me. Do you know of someone?"

Gage and Garrick exchange glances she can't read.

Someone stomps into the back door, and Starr's mouth drops. Another boy. Nobody pays attention to him, other than Starr, as he gets a bowl of stew and sits at the table. He studies her with the same intense gaze of Garrick, and she's pretty sure they're twins.

"Are there any other boys your hiding?" she asks, doing a quick count. Seven of them. Seven boys in one small house. Seven boys all alone with no parents.

"Nope, Giles is it. We're all here now." Gage still hasn't touched his stew.

"How old are you all?" She can't quite fathom a household so big, so full of only boys. It's so different from her life growing up alone. But Bard... he grew up in a household of brothers and sisters, although there was only five siblings in his family.

Gage sighs. "I'm almost eighteen. Garrick and Giles are sixteen. Then fourteen, twelve, ten, and six." He motions to each boy as he counts them off. "But we have more important things to discuss. Why do you need the Queen's Reject's help?"

His words bring her back to the threat she is facing. "I'm in danger and—"

"From who?" Gage throws up his hands like he's getting tired of this all. But she is also exhausted from trying to hide everything. The boys didn't have a negative reaction about the Queen's Rejects like that one woman had, and they obviously know who the group is.

But Gage said their mother was killed in a mine explosion, and Ivy threw their father into jail. There is no way they would support the queen after that.

Starr gathers her thoughts, taking a sip of stew to stave them off.

"I have angered the queen greatly. She ordered a huntsman to bring me to the woods and kill me, but he was a friend, and he let me go. He told me to look for someone among the Queen's Rejects because they would help me get in contact with somebody who can help me escape. That's it. That's everything." There, she's laid it all out for them. They either believe her, or they don't.

"Can she stay here with us, Gage? She knows how to skip rope." Gary laughs. "Well, kind of. And she can be like our mom?"

Garrick scoffs. "She's not old enough to be our mom."

Gage turns to Gary with a furious face. "You have a mother."

Gary's cheeks redden, and his face crumples. Starr promises to give him a hug later and thank him for thinking of her that way. The poor boy probably doesn't have the memories of his mother like his older brothers do.

"I can stay out in the shed. And tomorrow I'll be on my way if you tell me whom to go to." She doesn't want to impose any more than she already has.

Gage frowns. "There is nobody around here from the Queen's Rejects that can help you. We'll get word through the proper channels, but that will take a few days." He turns to the boy whose name she doesn't remember. "Geoff. Get your bed ready for her. Put a new blanket over it."

"No." She shakes her head vehemently. "I'm not taking Geoff's bed."

"It's not his bed," Gary blurts. "It's mine and Gaspar's too. And you can have it."

"No," she tries again. "You don't need to kick the three of them out of their bed. I can stay in the shed."

Gage rolls his eyes. "The shed is no place for a lady."

"Then the couch." She waves to the worn brown sofa across the room.

He gives her a look like she's a silly girl. "That's my bed. You can stay in the boys' room."

"Can I sleep in there too?" Gary brightens up. "On the floor next to the bed? I'll be quiet."

"No, dum dum." Geoff smacks Gary lightly in the shoulder. "She's a girl. She doesn't want you and your stinky gas in there."

"It's not as bad as yours." Gary glares at his brother.

"Yours are the worst," Gaspar says to Geoff, the first time Starr's heard him speak.

The three boys erupt into an argument about smells and gas and burps, and Starr sits back and laughs. Garrick grins at her, but Gage looks exasperated. He has been forced into being the adult for this family, and taking care of his siblings is a burden she's never had to deal with. But she's thankful to have found them and can't wait to get back to Bard.

Chapter Eighteen

Today is a good day. Starr is dead and will no longer get in the way of Ivy's happiness. She had wanted to watch the huntsman take care of Starr in the mirror yesterday, but her queenly duties kept her busy. Now she can get back to the work of finding a proper suitor.

"Mirror, Mirror on the wall, who is the most delightful woman of all?" Ivy stares into her reflection on the mirror and waits for Echo to return. Her image comes into focus, a grand smile on her face.

"There is no other more pleasant and noble than you, my queen."

"You are so right about that." Ivy giggles. "But now, on to more important business. I want you to see if you can find me the vision of my huntsman taking care of Starr." Ivy rubs her hands together in anticipation. Echo has never been able to see events from the past, but maybe it'll work this time.

"I will try, my queen." Echo sits back in her chair, tucks her hair behind her ears, and closes her eyes and concentrates. Her nose wrinkles after a few moments, she frowns, but then her face relaxes, and she tries again.

Ivy sits at her dressing table and makes sure her brush and new hand mirror and other things are in place. This is taking way too long. Not a good sign.

Echo opens her eyes. "I cannot find anything, but let me try again. I will concentrate harder on Starr rather than the huntsman." Echo's expression is blank at first, but then her eyes pop open. "My queen. I'm afraid I have bad news for you."

Ivy grips the edge of the table. "What is it?"

The picture appears in the mirror. Starr sits at a table finishing breakfast with several boys.

"It can't be." Ivy gasps. The huntsman killed her and buried her in the forest. He showed Ivy Starr's blood.

"It is."

Ivy leans closer to the mirror and blinks. This can't be happening to her.

"And what time will you be back from the mines, Gage?" Starr asks one boy.

"By eight. We can talk about things more," the oldest boy says.

"Stacey, Stacey." A young boy dashes to the table. "Are you done? I can take your plate, and we can skip rope again."

Starr laughs. "After we finish the dishes."

Ivy watches them talk for a bit, but then the picture wavers and disappears.

"I'm sorry. I lost it." Echo grimaces. This is not the time to be losing images.

"Bring it back," Ivy commands, narrowing her gaze.

"I can't, Your Majesty. You know I'm not all-powerful."

"Curses," Ivy thunders, slamming her silver brush on the dressing table. Starr is alive. The huntsman lied straight to her face. She should have confirmed with Echo that Starr was dead, but she never imagined her huntsman would defy her.

Ivy shoots to her feet and paces in front of the mirror. The boy works in the mines, which narrows down the area to search significantly. And there are three boys at the table and the younger one who ran up to Starr. A big family of boys shouldn't be hard to find.

That boy called Starr by the name of Stacey. A grin spreads across Ivy's face. Starr is hiding who she is, and now Ivy's plan will be so much easier to execute.

This morning when the maids report Starr missing, Ivy will order a search of the grounds to find her, but now everything has to change. Well, not that part, but they will have to add on.

"What will you do now?" Echo asks.

"I need to do some research. I will be back."

Ivy stalks to her door. She needs to get this day started so they can find Starr missing, and she wants to find one of her loyal squires.

She knows what to do about that traitorous huntsman, but she'll have to figure out where Starr is and then make a plan for her demise.

At breakfast, Ivy acts unconcerned that Starr is missing. The girl has probably gone for an early morning walk; at least that's what Ivy told the maids. And when they say they hadn't seen her since last night either, Ivy says Starr probably spent the evening with a man and then snuck to her room unseen.

Ivy sits at her dressing table once again, staring at the mirror as she brushes her silky blonde hair. It was not very hard to track down where the boys are. She had the first name Gage, a boy who works in the mines, and her Office of Taxation gave her just what she needed.

Someone knocks on the door, and after Ivy calls to enter, her maid escorts Miles, a squire, into the room. Miles lacks the intelligence of most of the young men, but he loves her and will do anything for her—just as it should be. She should have chosen him to kill Starr.

"My queen." Miles bows. "What is it I can do for you?"

"I need you to move my furniture around." She glances at the maid. "You may go now. Shut the door when you leave."

The maid scurries out of the room, and Ivy directs Miles to follow her to her sitting area by the windows. "Take a seat." Ivy points to the sofa, and he plops down. He knows something fun is about to happen to him. He's been in her room before.

Ivy lays a hand on Miles's thigh. "I have something very important to discuss. I need your help."

"Anything for you, Your Majesty."

"I have discovered something horrible. All morning I've been worrying about what I will do." Ivy blinks her eyes, trying in vain to bring out the tears. "Our Starr is gone."

"Gone?" Miles asks. He wouldn't have heard about the chatter from the maids about Starr not being seen yet, but he will soon enough.

Ivy turns her head and wipes her dry eyes. She can't quite muster the tears, so she needs to pretend. "I've uncovered a dastardly plot. One of my huntsmen has murdered our beloved princess, and he was planning to blame me. Me!" She huffs. "He was about to say I ordered the murder unless I gave him gold."

"No. Princess Starr is gone? How can that be?" Miles's voice sounds so sad. "She was so young and full of life. So pretty. And so soon after we lost the king. This will devastate the kingdom."

Ivy clenches her hands so she doesn't slap the dolt.

"I know." She matches his tone. "But we need to deal with this huntsman. I have no proof of what he did, and now he's trying to blackmail me. I need you to say that you saw him murder the princess." Ivy clasps Miles's hands in hers, willing him to agree. If he thinks too much about it, he will know that she would not need proof to convict the huntsman.

The queen's word is the law.

"Anything, my queen. Princess Starr deserves justice, and we can't let him get away with it."

Ivy releases a fake sob. "Thank you so much. This means much to me. I... I... don't know what else to do, and I'm so distraught over losing Starr. First King Adrian and now her."

She lets loose more loud sobs and collapses into Milo's strong arms. He holds her, stroking her hair. "There, there. It'll work out. I'll do whatever is needed of me."

Ivy knows he will, but she needs to seal the deal.

She continues to *cry* a bit more and then shuts off her sniffles and lays her head on his shoulder. "You are such a wonderful man. So loyal to the princess." Ivy runs her hand up and down his thigh, getting dangerously close to his manhood. He tenses up, and she imagines the excited thoughts running through his mind. It is a squire's biggest honor to be with the queen.

His trousers tent, and she makes her move, rubbing his manhood as she turns her face to kiss his.

Step one is done, and soon the huntsman who betrayed her will die, and then, so will Starr.

Chapter Nineteen

Starr watches Gage, Giles, and Garrick file into the house from their long day at the mines as she helps Garth and Geoff in the kitchen, getting dinner ready. At fourteen, Garth is more organized and is a harder worker than many of the servants at the castle. He does lessons with the younger boys, manages them as they do their chores, and when Geoff takes the boys outside to play, Garth starts on his big list of things to be done, which includes mending clothes.

Starr does whatever he asks today, and she hopes her help eases his burden slightly. She is helpless when it comes to the mending and cleaning, but she does her best. Geoff is even patient with her when he shows her how to gather eggs from the chicken coop.

This is her second full day with the boys, and she prays they bring back more information from the mines. They didn't see their supervisor yesterday, the one they need to speak with about the Queen's Rejects, but they said that was normal. He is only down with the workers every once in a while.

Maybe they got lucky today.

Gary runs over to the three eldest boys babbling about his fun day. The way he talks, Starr worries Gage might think she did nothing but sit around all day and play with him, but he is probably used to his little brother's enthusiastic stories.

Giles puts away the boys' bags and goes out back with the other two to wash their hands with the pump.

"We're ready to eat," Garth says, motioning to the table. A fatty piece of beef sits in the middle, one that Ivy would throw because it is such an inferior cut. Gage acknowledges her with a nod but doesn't say much more. Everybody else seems quiet, even Gary. It feels unnatural, like their eyes are on her, but they aren't ready to say what is needed.

"How was your day?" Giles finally says to her, his eyes shifting between her, Garrick, and Gage.

Starr opens her mouth to speak, but Garrick slams his fist on the table. "Just ask her."

Giles glares at his twin brother, and Starr bites on her lip. "Ask me what?"

Garrick turns his serious gaze on her. "What's your name? Where are you from?"

Starr remains quiet. They deserve the truth, but she isn't sure she can tell them. They won't believe her story anyway.

"I'm Stacey. I hail from—"

"Garrick," Gage snaps, "tell her your story."

Silence clogs the air, the only noise the boys shifting around. Garth pulls up a chair, and Geoff stands behind him. Even the young boys don't say a word.

"There was a hanging today," Garrick starts, his words calm and composed. A couple of gasps burst from the group of boys, but Starr doesn't notice who. "I traveled to town this afternoon to get medicine for Gaspar, and the town was abuzz."

"But it isn't Sunday," Starr says. They don't hold hangings on any other day.

"Who was it?" one boy asks.

Starr's stomach rolls. The Day of Penance is coming much too often.

Garrick holds up his finger to shush them. "This man they hanged had murdered the princess." He gives Starr a pointed look.

She lets out her own gasp. Starr isn't dead. "But…"

Oh no.

It can't be.

Ivy could not even wait the full week until the next Day of Penance; she had to hang the victim right away.

She's never done that before… not ever. So why would she now?

An uncomfortable mass settles in her belly. Somehow Ivy figured out David did not kill Starr, and now he paid with his life.

David, the kind and honorable man who only wanted to save her.

David, her friend.

Starr blinks back the tears. "It was a man named David, wasn't it?" Her voice trembles. There can be no other reason Ivy would do it so soon.

"Yes," Garrick replies.

"How'd you know that?" Gage asks. "You've been here with the boys all day, right?"

She can tell by the sound of his voice that his question isn't really a question. He is challenging her to tell the truth… They know.

Starr wipes her eyes and looks straight at Gage. These boys have done so much for her, provided her with food and shelter, and even allowed her to wear the clothes that once belonged to their mother.

"I am Princess Starr. Queen Ivy ordered her huntsman David to kill me. But instead, he gave me means to escape and sent me to find someone from the Queen's Rejects." And now David, her faithful friend, is gone.

Dead.

Murdered by Ivy.

She wants to scream, to hit someone, to run away and never look back.

"You're the princess?" Gary runs to the table. "You're Princess Starr. The Princess Starr who is so nice to everyone?"

Starr allows herself a small smile and pats the boy on his head. She tugs him over, wanting to hold on to the innocence inside him, and he crawls onto her lap. She doesn't want to think about David and what Ivy did to him. David's family has lost a loving and caring man, a man who would sacrifice his life for them.

"Yes, I am. And I'm sorry I lied to you. I was scared to tell the truth."

Gary frowns at her, eyeing her plainly braided black hair. "But you don't look like a princess. Where's your fancy dress and shoes? Where's your crown?"

Gage snorts, and Starr meets his eyes, then the eyes of the other boys. "I'm so sorry."

"We understand." Garrick nods solemnly.

Starr wraps her arm around Gary. "I don't wear a crown around. Only at balls or official events. But I do have a nicer dress in my bag. I was wearing it when David—" Starr's throat tightens. He gave his life to save her. "David brought me clothes more like yours so nobody would recognize me."

These boys welcomed her with open arms, providing her food and shelter and clothing. And safety.

"And everything you told us before was true then?" Gage asks.

"All but my name and who I was." Starr bites the side of her cheek, not wanting to ask. "What happened? What is the story?"

"A squire saw him kill you in the forest. He stood on the center stage and told what he witnessed. Queen Ivy stood next to him, crying over you. It makes sense now. David tried to proclaim his innocence and said that the princess was alive, and Queen Ivy yelled at him and ordered the hangman to do it even though it wasn't four o'clock."

Starr cringes, the image of David now added to the ones of Bronwen and Marshall Wallace.

"It's my fault he's dead." She will never forgive herself for being the reason David is gone. She should've made him come with her. They could've escaped together.

But he wouldn't have left his sister and family behind.

"But, Princess," Gage says, "it sounds—"

Starr holds her hand up to stop him. "Please, just Starr." She gives Gary a squeeze. "I want to be Starr."

"Okay, Starr then." Gage smiles softly. "I don't know if the queen was tying up loose ends or if she found out David let you go. But either way, she knows now because of what he said. You are still very much in danger."

Starr sucks in a hard breath, her grip tightening on Gary. Ivy will not stop until Starr is gone, and that means anybody helping Starr is in danger too.

She sets Gary on the floor and stands. "I will be out of here tonight. Give me time to get my bag together."

"No. You can't go," Gary whines.

"He's right. You can't leave." Gage spins his cup around in circles, staring at her. "You have nowhere to go."

"But I'm putting you all at risk, and I can't take the chance of you getting hurt." She can't bear to have one more death on her conscience, especially Gary or his brothers.

"We won't," Garrick agrees. "It's safer for you to stay here than be on your own. The queen probably has her men looking for you, and there are many of her supporters around. We're pretty concealed back here, and we rarely get visitors. So stay inside the house or in the backyard."

"Our supervisor should be in tomorrow," Giles adds. "He'll know what to do."

Starr slumps in the chair, her eyes and heart heavy. There's no point in hiding the rest of the story from them. "When you speak with him, tell him that Lord Emery, the Duke of Hillshire in Westray will help me. I was actually set to move to Westray with him. The queen did not know of our plan."

Giles pats her on the arm. "Don't worry. We'll get it figured out."

"What's it like to be a princess?" Gaspar asks quietly, filling the heavy silence.

It was good, up until her father died, and Ivy took over.

"Being a princess is fun at times, but it's also work." She closes her eyes for a moment. She did not know of real work until she came to be with the boys.

"Do you miss it?" Gary asks, throwing his arms around Starr and putting his head in her shoulder. His small, warm body provides much comfort.

"I do."

She must move on to her new life now, but she will make sure Gary and his brothers are taken care of after she is gone. She needs to get away though because if something happens to this little boy, to any of these boys, she will never forgive herself. And she already has one innocent death on her conscience.

She can't take any more.

Chapter Twenty

Ivy stands at the doorway, a basket of apples on her arm. She adjusts the worn skirt and hopes she can get out of here quickly and get home. The skirt and shirt itch her skin and have a fetid smell, and the shoes are terribly uncomfortable. She doesn't understand why the peasants wear clothes like these, but Echo said this is the best way to get to Starr. Trick her into taking poison.

She puts on her nicest smile despite the hatred brewing inside. These boys have committed treason, hiding Starr away from her. It shouldn't surprise her though, once she found out who their parents were. The mother died in a mining accident, and the father blamed Ivy for some ridiculous reason. He protested in the village and refused to go away until he was jailed for ignoring Ivy's orders. Another inmate beat him to death halfway into his sentence, which was good, because it opened up a spot in the increasingly overcrowded jail.

The door swings open, and a chubby-faced little boy stares at her.

"Hello, young man. I have apples for you." She gives him a sweet smile.

"Gary," an older boy sighs from behind the small one. "I told you to wait."

The door opens wider, and suspicious eyes meet hers.

"Hello," she repeats, keeping her gaze on the boy and not looking for Starr. "Would you like some apples?" She holds an apple out, and the impertinent little boy grabs it from her.

The older boy slaps the younger boy's hand. "Gary, please."

Ivy laughs. "Don't worry. I have many grandchildren myself. You go ahead, young man." She wipes her straggly hair behind her ear. She was horrified earlier when she saw her reflection: the gray hair, the wrinkles, the discolored skin. But it is necessary to perform this charade.

"We have no money to pay you, ma'am," the boy says apologetically. She's not surprised, considering the state of their pathetic home.

"Don't you worry. I know about your parents and how hard it is for you boys. I want you to have as many apples as you want."

A crunch escapes as the little boy bites into his apple. Ivy has to pay attention because she only has one poisoned apple, and Starr needs to eat it.

"I knew your mother. She was a wonderful woman." Ivy feigns sorrow for the boys' benefit.

"You did?" The older boy's eyes light up, and Ivy worries he might start asking too many questions. She pushes past them, walks to their table, and sets her basket down. Still no sight of Starr.

"She made a delicious apple pie." Ivy hopes the statement is true.

"She did." The boy nods, following her. The little one skips behind.

"You must remind me of your name, young man. Your mother talked of all you boys, but I could never keep track of who was who."

"I'm Gaspar."

"And I'm Gary," the younger one pipes up. She pats the boy on his head, trying to keep from cringing at his greasy hair. These boys need to be dunked in a tub and scrubbed with soap and water.

"How many apples would you like? You can have as many as you want." She slides the basket closer. "You tell me how many, and I will count them out for you."

Another door slams, and Ivy turns.

Starr.

A frowning boy rushes over. A boy who is disloyal to Ivy. The other two are young, but this boy is old enough to know what he is doing. Starr has turned her back on her kingdom, and Ivy, and she deserves no help from them.

"Who are you?" he asks. His head flips back and forth between Gasper and Ivy. Starr remains by the door, not moving. She wears a grungy brown shirt and skirt, and her hair is slipping out of the badly woven braids. She has fallen far from her throne—nobody deserves it more than Starr.

If only Lord Emery and all those others enthralled with her could see her now. They'd be disgusted.

"This is…" Gary's face wrinkles. "I don't know your name."

Ivy laughs lightly. "I am Mrs. Plante. Your mother was a friend of mine, and I was in the area and was talking with Mrs. Goodsen, and she told me what happened to your parents. I wanted to drop by apples for you boys. We have a big crop and won't be able to sell them all."

She was glad she'd spoken with the woman down the road. It gives her story more credibility.

"It's really sweet, Garth." Gary waves the half-eaten apple at his older brother. "Can you make a pie?"

Garth shrugs. "Maybe."

"Starr, Starr." Gary waves. "Come have an apple."

Yes, eat an apple, Ivy repeats silently.

Garth glares at his little brother. "Gary."

"Oh," the small boy says, and Ivy hides her gleeful smile. Even if she hadn't had Echo, these boys wouldn't be able to hide the fact that they have Starr here.

"Would you like an apple, my dear?" Ivy grabs the poisoned one, urging Starr silently to walk this way. She holds the shiny red apple out enticingly, and Starr creeps forward.

The middle boy—Ivy can't remember his name now—happily crunches on his apple, and Starr takes hers. Ivy ignores the urge to grab Starr and squeeze her throat.

Ewww—the putrid smell. The girl needs a bath more than the boys, and those blisters on her fingers. Does she have some sort of sickness? What might be causing them?

"Thank you," Starr says. That was at least one thing her father taught her: manners.

Ivy turns her back to Starr and begins removing apples from the basket, the younger two boys helping. "I told the boys they could have as many as they wanted." She smiles at the young one. "Didn't I?"

"Yes," he says with a full mouth.

Ivy hears the unmistakable sound of a crunch from behind her but keeps her focus on the table. "Mrs. Goodsen said to say hello. She said she hadn't seen your older brothers for a while."

If they check out Ivy's story, that part will be true. Ivy suffered through a half hour of tea and biscuits with the aggravating woman in her fetid home. And the tea was revolting, the biscuits hard.

"They work a lot," the middle boy says. Ivy can't remember their names anymore, not that it matters. Starr continues to take bites of the apple.

"They are good brothers." Ivy rolls her eyes inwardly. Fools more like it. Ivy wouldn't stick around and take care of her younger siblings. Her two sisters and her brother are spoiled brats who only pretend to like Ivy because she married the king. Ivy shifts to see Starr better.

"Would you like more apples?" Ivy motions to the ones left in the basket.

"No, we'd better leave some for somebody else." The older boy shrugs.

"No, no. You have them." Ivy sets two more down.

Suddenly, Starr is falling. Her head slams into the side of the table, and she thumps to the floor.

"Starr?" the little one yells as the older one rounds the table. He kneels next to her, and Ivy joins him.

"What happened?" Ivy asks. "Is she okay?" The time has finally come for the spoiled brat to die. She hides her gleeful smile as the boys crowd around, everybody chittering.

"Did you see her head hit the table?"

"That must've hurt."

"Why did she fall?"

Ivy cradles Starr on her lap, cackling silently. Starr is finally out of her life, once and for all. She's taken her last breath.

The oldest boy holds Starr's wrist at the same time he touches her forehead. "She must have fainted. Her forehead is hot."

Dopey boys. They don't know she's dead. Ivy better play along.

Tears gather in the middle boy's eyes. "Is she alive?"

"Yes," the one boy scoffs. "She just fainted."

"How do you know?" Ivy asks. Starr couldn't be alive after ingesting the poison.

He holds Starr's wrist. "Her heart's still beating, and you can see her chest moving."

Ivy stares down, and sure enough, Starr's chest is rising and falling very slowly.

Curses. She isn't dead.

"Gaspar. You need to run to the Langlees. Tell them we have a visitor who fainted and that they need to retrieve the doctor. They'll take the wagon to get him. And tell Geoff he should come home as soon as he can."

The middle boy pops to his feet. "Okay, I'll be back," he calls as he rushes for the door.

Ivy knows Starr hasn't fainted; the poison isn't strong enough in that apple. But she will stay here until the doctor arrives so as not to appear suspicious.

She has no idea how long Starr will be asleep, but she won't make this mistake again. She will devise a new plan, one that Starr nor the boys will survive.

Ivy stares in the mirror, her arms crossed. Echo should've known the poison wasn't strong enough or that the apple would dilute the effects. She will let it go this time.

"I'm one step closer to getting rid of that tramp, no thanks to you," Ivy says.

Echo grimaces. "I'm sorry, my queen."

"If you had suggested I have her drink the poison, it would've worked."

Still, the glorious image of Starr dropping to the floor after taking a bite of the apple repeats in Ivy's mind. Too bad she hadn't bumped her head harder.

"I'm unable to use the poison anymore. She is asleep and can't drink anyway, but even if she wakes, the boys will be on edge." Ivy sighs. The boys did not suspect she was involved luckily. "I cannot show up at their house again and entice her as I did before. But I have a better plan."

Ivy can't wait long because she'll risk Starr waking and escaping to another location. Not that Ivy can't find her wherever she goes, but traipsing across the countryside to get rid of her loathsome step-daughter is not something Ivy wants to be doing.

That double-crossing huntsman could not follow directions, but she knows someone who can. And, with this new plan, those traitorous seven will be punished too.

"I think it's time for a celebration. I will be back later, and we'll discuss what we can do with those boys who helped her." Ivy throws her drape over the mirror so Echo won't ask too many questions. She needs to work out a few details, and this time, she won't need Echo's help.

Chapter Twenty-One

Garth can't believe this is happening. A real live princess asleep in the bed. Somewhere deep down, he feels that it is his fault, but he shoves those thoughts away.

"This isn't natural." Gage stares at Princess Starr. Gary is curled up next to her, asleep because he is so exhausted from the late night and long day.

"It's been over twenty-four hours." Garrick paces in the bedroom, the other boys either sitting on the bed or floor or somewhere else.

"Gage. Gage," Geoff calls, running into the room and huffing for breath, a limp chicken hanging from his hand and Gaspar behind him. Gary shoots up in bed and rubs his red eyes.

"What happened?" Gage steps over and takes the dead chicken from Geoff.

"Six of the chickens are dead." He shrinks back.

"What do you mean dead?" Garrick shoots up and stares out the back window, and Garth joins him. Two chickens lay on the ground in front of the coop, but the others aren't visible.

Dead chickens.

Starr.

The apples.

The boys rush to the door to check out the scene, but Garth spins around. "Stop."

He debates whether to continue. They will all hate him. First Starr and now the chickens.

"I... I..." He clenches his fists to gather the courage he needs. "The apple yesterday. The one Starr ate from. She only took a bite, and I didn't want to waste it, so I cut it up and fed it to the chickens. And now they're dead."

"You think she was poisoned?" Gage folds his arms and stares with accusing eyes.

"Poison?" Gary asks in a meek voice. "Is she dying?"

"I'm sure she'll be okay," Giles says, but Garth worries that she might never wake up.

He looks to his feet. "What else could it be? Why would six of our chickens just die?"

"It's possible." Gage sighs. "The queen must have found Starr and hired this woman to poison her."

"It makes sense." Garrick glares at Garth. "It was that old woman. It has to be her. Why did you let her in?"

Garth can't face his brothers. The younger boys and their home are his responsibility when the older ones are gone. He should have sent the old woman on her way as soon as he saw that Gaspar and Gary let her in. All he needed to do was keep Starr safe until the mine supervisor could help her.

And now she's sleeping and won't wake up. They've tried everything, but nothing has worked.

"She talked about Mother and Father and Mrs. Goodsen," Garth blurts. "She brought apples, and she didn't hardly pay attention to Starr. I thought—"

"You are so dim," Garrick snaps. "You shouldn't have—"

"Garrick, enough." Gage watches Garth shrink farther into himself. "Any one of us could've made the same mistake."

"When will she wake up?" Gary raises his head, his bangs falling over his wide brown eyes.

Gage sits next to him. "I don't know. But Nigel will be back tomorrow, and he can help us out. Starr needs you right now. You need to check on her during the day when we're gone, and you can sit with her and tell her stories or do your tricks. Can you do that?"

Gary nods enthusiastically. "I can do that."

"Okay, good." Gage pats Gary on the shoulder and looks to Giles and Garrick. "When Nigel shows up, we need to discuss moving Starr's body. We don't know if it was a random act or if the queen was trying to kill her, but Starr is vulnerable here and should be brought somewhere safe."

A light murmur runs through the room, and Garth swallows back the lump in his throat, hoping neither the queen nor any of her minions do not return before they get Starr out of here.

Chapter Twenty-Two

This Sunday it will happen: a few days away. An explosion will blow up the house in an unfortunate accident, and it will burn down.

Ivy rubs her hands together. They will die at once, including Starr, and best of all, it will be on a Day of Penance. Nobody will know Starr is there, and none will know how those seven boys betrayed their queen, but Ivy will.

Someone knocks at the door, and Ivy looks up from her mirror to the maid. "What do you want?" she snaps. Of all the times to interrupt her, when she is thinking about the demise of those traitors.

The maid grips a rag tightly, like she's afraid to drop it. "Lord Emery is here to see you."

What does he want? He made his interest in Starr clear, but he must have traveled all this way to offer his condolences.

"Show him in," she gruffs and retreats to her sitting area.

A moment later, Lord Emery strolls in, a frown on his elegant face. He looks just as he had the last time she saw him, long black hair tied at his neck, and stunning brown eyes. He approaches her and bows. "Queen Ivy. I wish I could've visited under better circumstances, but it's nice to see you."

"Have a seat. Why are you here?" This man could have had her whole kingdom, and he threw it away on that little twit.

Lord Emery glances at the door, where the maid stands. "This information is private, but is of utmost urgency."

"Be gone." Ivy waves the maid away, who closes the door behind her. "Now, what information do you have that is so important?"

"I have a grave report to share, but first..." He drops to his knees. "I must apologize from the deepest part of my heart. When I was here, I..." His voice wobbles. "I let myself be seduced by the princess. Since the day I left, I have been going over my mistake. I was here, under your invitation, and I let her bewitch me."

He looks up with repentant eyes.

"Continue," Ivy says, keeping the scowl on her face.

"I tried to figure out why it happened." He wrings his hands. "There was another woman, a much more lovely and brilliant woman in this castle, and I was a dunce to ignore her." Lord Emery raises his gaze to hers. "I've questioned myself over how I could have been so blind. The princess is nothing compared to you. Half as bright, ugly in comparison, and I started to wonder if she cast a spell over me."

Ivy gasps. She's never considered the possibility, but no man could have been interested in Starr on their own. Somewhere she found someone to help her create a spell. It's all making sense now.

"It's not just that," Lord Emery continues. "She is not an honorable woman, and it pains me to remember the cruel words she said about you."

"And what did she say?"

"That you were driving this kingdom to the ground. That you are cruel and heartless. The statements are so ridiculous, and I should've walked away from her. The princess was a silly little girl, and you are a strong and striking woman. I think of all that I gave up, when I could have had you by my side."

Ivy clenches her fists. If she didn't already have a plan to get rid of Starr, she would've created one after this.

Lord Emery looks up at her from the floor, so pathetic, but so attractive.

"Do I have your forgiveness?" He rises to his feet. "Please, my queen. My life has been so lonely since I've left your side."

She can't blame the man for being spelled. Well, perhaps a little, but really, those stunning green eyes hold so much pain, and she wants to see him bright again.

"Of course I do."

He might make a good king, the way he kneels on the floor before her.

"Thank you so much, my queen. You have made me a happy man." He pulls over a chair and sits, his smile dropping. "But now I need to share the worst of my story with you." He tugs at his shirt, not meeting her eyes. "You may not be aware, but you have a number of disloyal subjects in your kingdom. Traitors who oppose your rule."

"Not true. My subjects love me." Yes, they have the occasional turncoat, like Marshall Wallace, but she can easily take care of them. And yes, the random protestors, those at the mines, and the small rebel groups. But those are few and far between.

"I wish that were true, my queen. But I've discovered a gang of seven who are hiding the princess and are working with others to take away your rule. That huntsman who claimed to kill her and that other man who saw it… He was lying. I believe he is working to hide the princess from you. That he is a part of this dangerous group who opposes you and wants to remove you from power."

Miles would never betray her, but Starr has worked against Ivy to stop her from making this kingdom into the place it should be.

"She's alive? And she is involved with some who want to form a revolt?" Ivy has to pretend she doesn't know Starr isn't dead though.

This has gone deeper than she imagined. Starr was probably working with Marshall Wallace and his daughter, which is why she was so upset after they died. And then she found these boys. Just because Ivy never witnessed them talking about being a part of that rebel group, doesn't mean they never did.

Starr's betrayal has no bounds. Ivy wants so badly to be close to that house when it blows up, but it is a Day of Penance, and she must be here.

"I'm afraid so." Lord Emery clears his throat, his face grave. "We must find the man who claims to be a witness. What is his name?"

"Have you seen her? Where is this place?" She must keep Lord Emery off track.

"No, my queen. I had a spy check out the story for me. But they are protective of her and are keeping her hidden. You must find her, arrest her, and convict her. Her treason deserves the most horrific of deaths."

"You are correct. We shall send the royal forces to that house and arrest them all." A smile spreads across Ivy's face at the wonderful image of Starr being led away in chains. Too bad it won't happen.

"Just as important, we must find the squire who has colluded with her. What is his name?"

Ivy waves him off. "I will have a team arranged by Monday to search for her. We will find her."

Except that Starr will be dead by Sunday.

"And the man who lied?"

"I will take care of him." She shutters her grin. After Miles disposes of Starr and the others, she can tie up that loose end too. Although she will miss bedding him. "We will send them to jail for their traitorous ways." Ivy glances at the clock. "It's getting close to dinner time. Clean yourself up. It's been a long journey, and you must be tired. We'll have dinner and enjoy a quiet evening together."

"I look forward to it, my queen." Lord Emery takes her hand and kisses it, then sweeps out of the room.

At dinner, he sits close to her, and they talk and laugh and enjoy each other's company. A maid opens their second bottle of wine, and Ivy sends her off so the two can speak alone.

Lord Emery has stunning eyes, and he can barely take them off her. He is a true gentleman.

"Let's have a toast," Lord Emery says.

"We already made one." Ivy giggles.

"But this is a new bottle. It deserves a toast too."

"Then I shall make a toast." Ivy holds up her glass. "To us and our new life together." Yes, Lord Emery will fit in wonderfully to her life. "And it all starts Sunday."

"To us." He clinks glasses with her and takes a sip. "But what is happening Sunday?" His voice is so strong and seductive, and she can't wait to get him into bed.

"I don't want to talk about Starr anymore. Let's just say that Sunday will be a glorious day."

"As you wish, my queen." His beautiful lips grin at her, and she melts a little more inside.

Yes, tonight will be a fun night.

Chapter Twenty-Three

"Pour me another glass of wine." Ivy rolls over in bed, her heart racing, her body flushed. Lord Emery is a wonderful and attentive lover. If she is to marry him, she might not need the attention of the squires.

Well, she will still invite them to her room sometimes. They would miss her too much.

Lord Emery hands her the glass, and she props herself up onto her pillows and takes a sip. He did not allow them to consummate their relationship, but she can wait for that part.

"I was thinking, my queen, how nice it would be to serve justice on the princess and those other traitors on the Day of Penance. Instead of waiting until Monday, we should send a team out right away."

"Oh no." Ivy scoffs. "Sunday has too many things going on. Monday is much better."

He nods solemnly. "Can I be there when you arrest her and hang her? She has not only hurt you and our kingdom but also me. I want to see her pay for her crimes."

"You may." Ivy runs her hand through Lord Emery's dark hair, and he scoots closer to her body and runs his hand up and down her belly. She giggles. Except Starr won't be there Monday to be arrested.

A shame, really. Ivy would love to see Starr hanging from a rope.

Should she tell Lord Emery of her plans? He will definitely appreciate her cunning.

"Tonight has been wondrous," he says. "You have fulfilled every one of my dreams." Lord Emery's touch makes her flutter inside, and she lies still as he traces circles on her belly. "No woman could measure up to you, and there is no doubt that you are deserving of the title of queen."

"I am," she agrees. "It's hard to believe that if I hadn't met Adrian, he would have died and left the kingdom to that trollop."

Lord Emery frowns. "Where would we be now? Much worse off, that's for sure."

"Yes, yes." She nods. "And I might not have got here if not for the mirror."

"Mirror?" His brows rise.

Oh, the wine must be talking. She probably shouldn't tell him about the mirror, but if he is to be her husband, he will find out anyway.

"I have a magical mirror. Inside is a woman who offers me advice. Echo is like an advisor."

"A woman in the mirror." Lord Emery laughs. He doesn't believe her.

She narrows her eyes. "I'm serious. If you must know, I've known about Starr all this time. Echo showed me a while ago. I'm the one responsible for her falling into a deep sleep."

"What are you talking about?" He sits up and takes her hand. "She's in a deep sleep?"

"Your spies do not know everything." Ivy grins. "I disguised myself and offered her a poisoned apple, but instead of killing her, it only put her to sleep."

"You did?" Lord Emery's face is full of awe. "How did you do it?" He reaches over and grabs his glass of wine. "Wait, you know where she is already? We must arrest her."

"I do. The mirror has shown me." Ivy laughs. "And the best part yet? We won't need to arrest her."

"What do you mean?"

Ivy is dying to spill the story. Only Echo and Miles know the plan.

"Sunday, the house she's at will explode. They will be home, and since Starr's body is there, she'll disappear into that big blast too. The plan is all set up, and my squire is already preparing everything."

Lord Emery blinks at her, and for a moment, she regrets telling him. Then his smile grows into laughter.

He sets his glass to the side and kisses her. "You are a genius, my queen. They deserve it after how they betrayed you. I never could have thought of something so clever, and I can't be more proud of having you as my queen as I am right now."

"You're so sweet." She pats his shoulder. "I've gone back and forth over what to do. The kingdom should know how their princess betrayed them, but we already hanged the huntsman for killing her, so it'll be much simpler to get rid of her this way."

She is about to push Lord Emery's head to her womanhood, but he pulls away, his eyes bright. "Can you show me this mirror? I've never heard of such a thing. How does it work?"

Ivy glances across the room.

"Is it over there?" Lord Emery asks, sliding off the bed and striding away with no clothes. He still does not believe her.

She leads him to the mirror and pulls off the black drape. "Mirror, Mirror," she calls.

Echo's image appears. "My queen, what can I do for you?" She spies the naked Lord Emery standing next to her and gapes. Perhaps the two should have dressed, but he doesn't seem to be bothered by his nakedness.

"Lord Emery wanted to see how the mirror works. He will be spending a lot more time with me." She reaches for his hand and squeezes. He squeezes back.

"Show him a picture of Starr," she orders.

"But, my queen—"

"I said to show us," she snaps.

An image forms of the princess lying in a bed, a white cloth draped over her. Lord Emery gasps. "Are you sure she isn't dead?"

"Not yet." Ivy giggles, watching as a boy passes by Starr. He sits on a chair next to her bed, speaking softly. "They do that sometimes. Talk to her like she will wake up."

Lord Emery studies the mirror, then shakes his head. "How do you get these images?"

The picture of Starr disappears, and Echo's face fills the space. "From me."

"Yes, from her." Ivy gives Echo a wave. "I ask her to find me the pictures, and she does."

"Can you see events from the past and the future?" he asks Echo.

"Only things that are currently happening," Ivy replies. "It's very useful for keeping my enemies in check. Echo has served me well, helping to root out those traitors. She even led me to the huntsman who betrayed me."

Ivy has to show Lord Emery the power behind the mirror. "Echo, find the older boys taking care of Starr. I want to see what they're up to."

"Yes, my queen."

Lord Emery sweeps in between Ivy and the mirror. "You are amazing. This is amazing." He kisses her lips and runs his finger between her thighs. "This whole idea makes me want you more."

Ivy melts into his kiss, the desire stirring inside her again.

"I need to show you something," Echo calls.

Lord Emery kisses Ivy harder, his hands teasing her burning skin.

"Your Majesty," Echo says again, more urgently.

"I want you," Lord Emery says, his hot breath hitting her ear. "But not in front of her."

"Then throw up the drape," Ivy murmurs.

Lord Emery positions the cloth, the words of Echo getting muffled. Then he sweeps Ivy into his arms and carries her to bed. He tosses her down and scrambles on top of her.

Then he takes her one more time.

Chapter Twenty-Four

Bard is awake in bed, counting the minutes. He spent an hour bedding Queen Ivy, but now she's sleeping silently at his side. Her naked breasts rise and fall, the moonlight streaming in the uncovered windows. In a house in the woods, Princess Starr lies sleeping under the same moon.

In less than two days, that house and everybody inside will be gone.

He rolls off the bed and marches off to use the washroom, filled with disgust for what he had to do last night. Ivy's loose lips let out some secrets in the early evening, and he had no choice but to get her drunk and perform for her. He loathes what he had to do to get here, but it was necessary to gain her trust.

When he returns, he pauses at the draped mirror. Who knew such a thing could exist. And who is that woman, Echo, on the other side? He touches the gilded frame, and it feels as real as anything.

He sits next to Ivy—she appears so angelic in the moonlight. Even though she is a few years older than him, she has retained her beauty, and most men would consider themselves lucky to be chosen by the queen.

He is not one of them.

Bard reaches under the bed and pulls out his bag. Starr might never wake again, but he will do everything in his power to revive her, or keep her safe forever.

His fingers touch the wooden handle, and he grasps the small sharpened knife. Evil like this does not deserve to live, and he hopes Starr will understand.

He slices the knife across Ivy's neck, and her eyes open for a second but quickly fall closed. The blood gushes out of the wound, and he says a silent prayer asking for forgiveness.

Snuffing out a life isn't something he takes lightly, but there is no other choice. Ivy's dark reign needs to end. He doesn't even want to think about those boys, the youngest being only six, of them losing their lives to this woman.

He leaves the knife at the bed, dresses, and trudges to the mirror. When he arrived at the castle, his hope was to figure out where Ivy got her information so he could then keep Starr safe, but he never imagined a magic mirror is the one helping her out.

Bard yanks off the drape. "Mirror, Mirror," he calls, and Echo immediately appears.

"I know who you are." She points her thin finger at Bard. "Where is the queen?"

"Who are you?" Bard demands. Is this woman located somewhere in the kingdom, or does she live in the mirror, some magical entity?

"I am the queen's faithful servant. Who are you to question me?" Her gaze is hard as stone.

"And you've been helping her spy on everybody?" Ivy has always been one step ahead of her enemies, and now he knows why.

"I don't spy. I flush out the snakes who are trying to overthrow my queen." Her triumphant glee puts him even more on edge.

Bard's hands fist up. The two have been responsible for so many deaths, so many innocent lives lost. Ivy probably never would have created so much misery if not for her mirror.

"Your actions are as heinous as the queen's."

"Queen Ivy? Where are you, my queen?" Echo calls frantically and lets out a gasp. "What have you done with her?"

"She is gone." Bard steps to the side to give Echo a view. "Dead. Now tell me who you are and where you are?"

"Never," Echo snarls. "You will pay for what you've done."

"And so will you?" Bard growls. He picks up a silver hairbrush and smashes it into the mirror. Several large pieces fall to the dressing table, and the woman's face is gone.

Bard rushes to his bag. He should've pushed harder to get the name of the squire from Ivy, but if he'd asked much more, she would've become suspicious. That man is still out there, and now Bard's only focus is to save Starr and the seven boys.

These past few days have been so up and down. He'd been waiting to hear word from Starr so he could return to bring her to Westray, but then his heart broke when she was murdered by the man she said was a friend. The man she invited to come with her.

And then the message from a contact in the Queen's Rejects who said she was alive and in hiding. They hadn't said she'd fallen into a deep sleep though, and now in his anger, he may have ruined the one chance he had to find out how to wake her. He shouldn't have broken the mirror.

But he needs to save Starr.

Bard stares at the bed. He betrayed Starr in order to trick the queen, but it had been necessary. If he hadn't discovered how Ivy got her information or her real plan, Starr would very likely have ended up dead.

And Bard might've been right there with her when that man blew up the home.

He'd done what was necessary, and he might have taken one life, but now he could save the others.

"Wake up." Bard shakes the maid's shoulder gently, and Melinda jerks awake.

She blinks up at him from her warm bed in her room in the maid's quarters. He has snuck in to talk to her. She might know the name of the squire who is helping Ivy.

And he needs her help.

"Lord Emery?" Melinda squints at him.

He kneels next to her bed. "Yes, it's me. I need your help. Princess Starr needs your help."

"Princess Starr is gone." Deep sorrow fills Melinda's voice.

"She is not. She is hidden away in the forest, but she is in danger. Ivy tried to kill Starr once, but David didn't follow her orders, and now Ivy has devised a plan to blow up the home where Starr is hiding. A home of innocent children."

Melinda rubs at her eyes and sits up, pulling her blanket around her. "I don't understand."

"Ivy is behind everything. She ordered David to kill Starr, but he sent her to safety, so she framed him. He did not kill Starr." They need to set their plan in motion. It won't be long until a maid finds Ivy dead, and chaos will erupt.

Melinda lays a hand on her heart. "I knew that boy could not hurt her. They were close." She squeezes her eyes shut and sighs. "And now he's gone."

"He is, and so is Ivy. But not the squire she's ordered to kill Starr. That's why I need your help. To save Princess Starr."

"Queen Ivy?" The disbelief spills from her eyes.

"Yes, she's dead." He doesn't want to explain how right now, but she will soon find out. "We need to save the princess. Do you know who the man is that Ivy has ordered to kill her?"

Melinda shakes her head sadly.

"Are there any squires or huntsmen she has special relations with?" Most likely Ivy was bedding the man too.

"She has relations with many of them."

Bard grits his teeth. This will be impossible. "Then I need to return to the house to save her and the children. But we can't allow word to get out that Queen Ivy is gone." Today is Saturday and tomorrow Sunday. The day the man will blow up the house. "We must keep the queen's death quiet. Do you think you can get to her room first and keep the others away? Maybe say she is sick?"

"I will do my best." A determined look falls upon Melinda's face. He is putting her in danger too. If someone discovers the body, she will be blamed, and arrested and possibly tortured before everything is sorted out.

Thank goodness the castle is quiet at night, no servants roaming the halls.

"Before I leave, I will help you arrange the body so she looks like she's sleeping. You must keep everyone away from her."

It is imperative that they return Starr to the castle before chaos erupts and people try to claim the right to the crown.

"I have others who can create diversions. Please let me speak to them, and then I will join you in her room." She grabs Bard's hands, clasping them tightly. "Please save Princess Starr."

"I will," he promises, one he can't keep. The squire helping the queen might start things early if he has the opportunity.

And what if they don't catch him? Even if Starr and the boys are safely removed, this man might not give up his quest.

"And I promise to return for you once we have the princess out of harm's way." He hopes he sounds reassuring, but he doesn't know what will happen.

"Be safe, my lord." She bows her head, and he pats her shoulder.

"You too."

Chapter Twenty-Five

Bard stares down at the exquisite beauty, her body lying peacefully in the bed, her raven hair framing her stunning pale face. He wants so badly for her green eyes to open and gaze upon him. It is not long ago that they shared a stolen kiss, that he'd watched a broken woman share her fears about the ones she loved, about the kingdom she loved. He should have whisked her away that day.

He strokes the back of her warm wrist and then lays his hand over hers, entwining their fingers together. That day at the pond wasn't the place to bring up the Queen's Rejects and their fight against her queen, but he knows she would have been supportive of them once she got away from Ivy. He had not been involved in their fight, but he would have for Starr.

The point is mute now though.

The night is still dark, but light will be here soon, and they need to remove Starr and the others. Four of the eldest boys stare at him as he sits next to Starr on the bed. Four of Ivy's targets.

"How will you wake her?" the eldest boy, Gage, whispers.

"I'm not sure." Bard doesn't know how to stop a sleeping spell. They will have to search for someone who could reverse the effects since they don't know how long it'll last. He squeezes Starr's hand again. She has to wake up: he can't imagine his life without her.

And now he is so close to losing her.

"What will we do?" Giles asks.

"We need to be gone before daylight. After I bring you boys and Starr to a safe home, I will find Nigel, and we can watch for the man who is coming." He hasn't yet met Nigel, the man who contacted him about Starr, but that is his next step.

"I'm not leaving her," Garth says, the boy, he was told, who let her stay when she showed up at his door.

"Me neither," another says, but Bard doesn't look up. His heart swells. In a matter of days, these boys have become loyal to her.

"Then you will all stay together." He runs his fingers along the back of Starr's delicate wrist. She looks dead, except for the rise and fall of her chest. Ivy did this to her. "You are allowed to each pack one bag. You must get the things for your youngest brothers. We will wake them before we leave. The less commotion, the better. Do you know of a safe place, or do we need to find Nigel?"

"I know of a home," Gage says. "We will be safe there."

Bard grabs Starr's hand. "I must stay behind, but I trust that these boys will care for you. I will see you after we find the scoundrel Ivy has sent."

He leans down and gives her a quick kiss on the lips. He prays it won't be long until Starr brightens his world again.

Her body shifts underneath his, and a small moan slips from between her lips. Bard almost jumps back.

"Starr?" He grasps her hand once again, and her eyes flutter. A commotion rips through the room, and the boys push against him and the bed, calling her name too.

Starr's green eyes blink open and stare at him. "Bard?" she chokes out.

"Starr, you're awake?" a brother calls, and she turns. Her gaze passes over each of the boys.

"What happened? Why are you here?" She glances at the dark window. "Why am I here?"

Bard's heart skips a beat. She has lost her memory.

"Queen Ivy tried to kill you, and—"

"I know that. But how did you get here? How did you find me? And why are you all surrounding my bed in the middle of the night?"

Bard tells her of the queen's new plan, leaving out the part that Ivy is dead. It's not something that can be discussed around the boys yet. "We must get you and the boys out of here so that we can lay a trap for the squire who means to hurt you."

"But if he shows up today or tomorrow, he will see that nobody is here, and he will leave."

"We will catch him."

"But you might not," she argues. "I must stay here so that he comes out of the shadows. Otherwise you might never see him."

"No." Bard crosses his arms. "You are the qu—" He almost admits the truth. "You are too important. We can't risk it."

"I'm not leaving." Her arms fold to match his. She has a strength that will serve her well in her new position, but he needs her to listen to him this one time.

"And if Starr doesn't leave, then I'm not either," a brother pipes up.

Bard turns to stare at the boy who is still a few years away from being an adult.

"Garth, you must," she admonishes him.

"I'm not either," Gage says, and the two other brothers agree.

"But if something goes wrong, he might hurt you. I don't know what he'll do." Her voice has turned to pleading, but it's not working on the boys. They shake their heads and argue more with her.

She has no choice. She must accept their assistance and face this problem together. These boys are so strong, so willing to fight.

"We're not leaving, Bard." The determination in her voice matches her face.

"We can send off the younger three." Gage nods along. "We must stay here so he knows he has the right place. We will stay inside and make noise so he hears us. But Starr is right. We can't risk him leaving because he finds the house empty."

Bard doesn't want to smile, but he can't help it. This majestic woman is honorable and courageous, as are these young men.

"Then you shall stay," he says, "but I will stay here with you."

"No, you will not." She puts her hand up. "Whoever it is might recognize you. We will keep weapons here."

"We have guns," Giles says. "And we know how to use them."

114

"We can protect ourselves." Gage sets his arms over Giles and Garrick's shoulders, and Giles links arms with Garth, the determination and strength showing in each of their faces.

There is no point in arguing. Bard will not win.

Chapter Twenty-Six

So much has happened to Starr in such a short time. She has so many questions for Bard, but he needed to take the three boys and get them to safety.

The whole day passes with no sign of the assassin. Despite promising not to go outside, Gage, Garrick, and Giles all do, but they make Garth remain indoors. And they don't allow Starr too close to the windows.

Garth takes another bread pan out of the oven, and Starr breathes in the wonderful scent. Garth laughs. "Maybe we can entice the man with our bread."

They've spent the last few hours baking, so bored, even though there is much they can do around the house.

"We'd better save some for Gary." Starr wipes down the counter with her wet rag. She misses the three youngest boys. Geoff's unending patience as he helps her through her chores. Gaspar's curiosity at her old life. And Gary's energy and passion.

He cried when they sent him away before the morning light arrived, and they did not allow him to say goodbye to her, but Gage thought it best that he didn't know she was awake as he might not want to leave.

"What happens after this?" Garth asks. Giles glances over from the window where he watches Gage and Garrick outside. The sound of another log being split flies through the window. After Bard left, she and the boys agreed that they needed to carry on as much as normal, especially without the youngest boys here. Bard will be so angry that they did not listen to him.

"They will catch the man, and he will be sent to jail." Starr wrings out her rag, hoping for the best.

"No, I mean, what about us? What about you?"

Me. The kingdom. Her former kingdom.

The pressure of it overwhelms Starr. In the few moments before he left, Bard explained that Ivy is dead, and that Melinda is doing her part to keep the story from being discovered until Starr is safe.

Melinda.

Starr folds another towel from the pile of laundry. Melinda is in danger too. So many lives in danger, so many lives lost.

And now Starr will be queen. She will be responsible for cleaning the mess that Ivy has created. One part of her wants to sneak off to Westray with Bard, but she can't abandon her homeland now. It will erupt in chaos once Ivy is discovered dead. No doubt many people will step up to fight for the crown. Some may be honorable, but others will be just as Ivy was, ruthless and cold-hearted.

And she can't risk her kingdom to those people.

"Starr?" Garth says, and she looks up from her oddly folded towel. He is as strong as his brothers, the first to demand to stay with her. He is a courageous young man.

"Queen Ivy has disrupted this kingdom, but she is now gone. I will be taking her place, and I hope that I can do our people justice." She spies Giles pretending not to listen, but his gaze is no longer trained outside.

"But what will happen to us? Gage and Garrick and Giles have missed several days of work. Their jobs probably won't be there when they get back." Garth swallows hard, and Starr sighs. He is still a boy. He isn't worried about the kingdom or the others. He is worried about his brothers, about their lives and how they will take care of each other. How they will eat; how they will survive.

She glances over to Giles, who is now watching them with curiosity. He is yet a boy too, only sixteen. These boys deserve their childhood back.

Starr takes the pan of bread and runs a knife around the edges now that it has cooled enough to touch. "Well, that is up to you. Your brothers have proven they can take care of you, and they will no matter what. You, as a family, can choose to stay here. Or if you'd like to move closer to me, you can sure do so." She looks at Garth with a smile. "We have a few extra rooms at the castle too."

Garth bites on his lip, a gleam in his eyes. "Do you think we can have our own room?"

Giles snorts, and Starr laughs. "We don't have *that* many bedrooms. Let's start with your own bed. How about that?"

"Deal." He sticks out his hand, and they shake. "No going back on your word now."

"I won't." She laughs again, hopeful to have light and laughter in the castle.

The door slams, and Starr jumps.

Gage looks between the three of them, his face red. "Stay away from the window. Garrick spotted movement in the woods."

"What's he doing out there?" Starr resists the urge to peek out the window and call Garrick inside. This man could attack the boy. Why didn't they listen to Bard? It was so unwise of them.

"It would look weird if we both ran off. He is finishing with the log and will come inside. It's getting close to sunset soon."

Starr scans the window, her heart thumping, but can't see much into the yard. Bard and the other men are hidden well.

"Bard will keep us safe," she says.

A small murmur echoes around the room, but none of them know how many men he has, or if it's just him watching for the assassin. It has to be more though. The boys' supervisor is a member of the Queen's Rejects, and there must be more.

The shadows will soon be deep, and whoever Bard has out there watching and waiting in the dark will be in as much danger as she and the boys.

Such a rash decision.

But it's too late now. And she must not show the boys her doubt.

"We should go upstairs to the bedrooms," she says.

"No." Gage shakes his head, and the door opens again. Garrick strolls inside, and Gage waits for the door to shut before continuing. "If he is sneaking around the house, we will hear him down here."

"Do you think his plan is to set up explosives inside the house?" Garth asks his oldest brother.

"I don't know."

The room falls silent. They must try to act normal now until they get the curtains closed.

"How about bread?" Starr says with fake positivity.

"I'm starving." Garrick rushes over to the loaf Starr has removed from the pan and pulls off a piece before she can cut it. She can't help but laugh, despite the danger outside. These boys will be okay.

But will they? Ivy has gone this far to rid Starr from her life, and others may follow her lead. They just need to get through these few days, and then Starr can move the boys somewhere safe if needed.

Chapter Twenty-Seven

The light flips on in the room, and footsteps race across the floor.

"Starr. Starr."

A small body slams into her, jolting her. "Starr. You're awake. They said you were awake."

"Gary, you're not supposed to be here." Starr wraps his arms around the young boy and hugs him. "How did you get here?"

Gary gives her a smug look, and his brothers start rising. An unfamiliar man rushes into the house, and Starr jumps in front of Gary.

"It's okay," Gage says, rubbing his eyes. "This is Tillis."

The man huffs and puffs, leaning on his knees. He catches sight of Starr and straightens. "Your Highness." He bows. "I apologize. Gary took off from our place, and I couldn't catch him. He is quite quick."

"Gary," Gage snaps. "You were not to tell anybody she is the princess."

Gary's lip quivers, and Starr sits and takes his hand in hers. "You shouldn't have left."

"But I heard Geoff tell Gaspar you were awake. I wanted to see you." His body slumps, tears filling his eyes.

"I know, and you will. Soon. But you need to return with Tillis."

"But I can stay here too. I can protect you." His eyes plead with her, but Giles pulls him away.

"Sorry, buddy. We'll see you soon." Giles hands a protesting Gary over to Tillis, who takes him out the door.

Not long after, they start their day, and it drags ever so slowly. Starr completes the tasks on her list, hoping Bard and his men find the man soon.

Mid-afternoon, they hear the clomping of horses coming down the road. Giles squints out the window, gripping the sill. "It's a group of men. That looks like a royal carriage."

Everybody runs to the window and peers outside. Not one, but two carriages arrive in the yard, and at least ten or more single riders on horses.

Starr eyes the uniforms of the men, dark green jackets and trousers with orange trim. The Royal Guard. Most of the group are civilians though.

"That's Sheriff Chambers. What's going on?" she asks.

Shouts erupt from the men, and the procession stops. Nobody in the house moves. Not even when Starr spies Bard marching up to the sheriff. They all talk, and he points to the house, nodding. Then gives a wave to them.

Starr rushes outside, the boys following, and approaches the group. The men snap to attention when they see her, and a few gasp. She doesn't look like a princess with her simple braids and her well-worn brown shirt and skirt. No shoes either, since they've run out of the house so quickly.

Sheriff Chambers turns, his mouth askew. "It's true." He rubs his eyes like he is unable to trust them but then offers a small bow. "Princess Starr. I mean, Your Majesty. You are alive. I didn't believe it until just now."

Starr freezes.

Your Majesty. That is the name for the queen. But she is the queen now. She knows that.

The boys and the chattering men push in a circle around her.

"Yes, Queen Starr is alive," Bard says, clasping onto her arm. "She has been hiding in this safe house."

"Well, I'll be." The sheriff scratches his chin and studies her. Starr's cheeks flush at the scrutiny. She does not have the dignified appearance of a queen, but she will behave like one.

"Why are you here?" Starr asks. Many new faces swarm around her, all full of curiosity, but she recognizes a couple, even if she does not know their names.

"Your Majesty." Oliver appears at her side, and she gapes at the steward who served not only Ivy but also her father and mother. "Thank goodness you are okay."

"We need to get you home," Sheriff Chambers says.

"What happened?" Starr tries again. Gage steps next to her, and she can't help but appreciate the young man and how he's kept her safe.

The sheriff glances at the gaggle of boys for the first time and then to Starr. "The queen was murdered, and things are getting chaotic. I was told that you were alive and in hiding."

"You must return to the castle to establish your rule," Oliver says. He motions to the carriage, and she starts to walk over but then stops.

"Bard," Starr calls. "The boys. The man…" The one who wants to assassinate her. His plans are to blow up the house today. She can't leave the boys.

"You need to leave. They will be removed from the house, and we will continue our watch. We can bring them to the castle too. I will speak with them to find out their wishes."

Starr's heart plummets. The man is probably long gone for now, but he might try again.

No, he undoubtedly will try again. He could easily be one vying for power now.

"I want—" she starts.

Bard holds up a finger to shush her, staring off over her shoulder. Starr turns but sees nothing unusual among the men.

"You there." He points to a man in ragged clothes. "You were not with the caravan earlier."

"No, sir. I saw the commotion and wanted to follow along. I wanted to be there when they found the princess." His tunic and trousers are dirtier than the rest, and he sort of hides between two men.

Bard's body tenses, and she remains quiet alongside him.

"Where did you come from? I didn't see you until now," another man asks.

"I was behind you," he stutters.

"No," a uniformed royal forces guard pipes up. "I was at the end of the group the whole time, and you never passed me. You've been in front of me this whole time."

Oliver takes a few steps to the side and frowns. "What are you doing here, Miles? You were not authorized to join us."

The young man, Miles, meets Starr's gaze, and he pulls out a revolver. He points it at Starr, and the crowd falls silent. There's a deadly click, and a scream smacks her ears. A shot rings out, and someone tackles Starr. She crashes to the ground.

Yelling and screaming men flash around her, and she rolls aside. Garth hunches over, his face pinched tight. A dark red splotch stains his shirt, spreading across the blue material.

"Garth!" Starr squeals, scrambling up on her knees. His brothers crowd around as he gasps for breath, his face pale.

"We need help?" Gage yells into the noise-filled air.

"It hurts," Garth whines, tears in his eyes.

"Don't worry. You'll be fine." She squeezes his knee, and he winces. The boys get pulled apart, and someone whisks Garth away. She tries to see where he's going, but Oliver is pushing her towards a waiting carriage. She is stuffed inside, Oliver hopping in behind her. The carriage door slams, and they race off down the driveway.

Starr wrings her hands, staring at the trees, unable to see the house. This is her fault. Garth was shot because of her. The blood. There was too much soaking his shirt. She swallows at the lump in her throat. She can't allow herself to not believe he'll be okay.

The boy has done so much for her; he taught her things she didn't know how to do, he welcomed her into his home—well, after that first day. He made her a part of his life, and now he may lose his because of her actions.

A lone tear slides down Starr's cheek and splashes onto her hand. She will never forgive herself if Garth dies.

Chapter Twenty-Eight

Starr can hardly believe a week has passed since Garth was shot, since she almost lost her life.

She stares at the large crowd gathered in the town square. It's the Day of Penance, and she has a ruling to make. Miles, the squire who caused her so much pain, stands in the corner of the stage, flanked by two guards. The same stage that has been the site of so many deaths.

A hush falls over the waiting crows as she steps to the edge of the stage.

"My people." Starr raises her hands and smiles. Her people. It's so hard to imagine. After Ivy came along, Starr pushed aside the idea of being their queen. They were her father's subjects, and Ivy's subjects, but never hers.

"My people," she says again. "Thank you for joining me on this Day of Penance."

Bard catches her eye, and a wave of confidence falls over her.

"We have been through a lot these last few years, and things have not been good. I make this promise, in front of you all, that I will do everything I can to make this kingdom the place it once was."

She is so new, and she knows she'll make mistakes, but she has many of the advisors by her side that once served her father, advisors Ivy disposed of.

"Today, I am handing down a sentence, but it is the last." A gasp rips through the crowd. "The former queen was involved with things she had no business taking over, but I will return control over all cases, even the most serious ones, back to the magistrates where they belong. I will do that after today."

She turns to Miles and motions the guards to bring him forward. He shuffles over, his head down. He has not once looked at her since he tried to kill her. He has not apologized for one thing he has done.

"Miles Abbott, you are sentenced to life in jail for your crime of treason. Your life has been spared, but that life will be spent in a cage where you belong."

There has been so much death in Starr's life, deaths that never should have occurred, and she will not be responsible for any more.

"Do you have anything you'd like to say for yourself?"

Miles's dour face remains frozen, and he rubs his toe over a small hole in the wooden stage. Starr waits a few moments, waves for them to remove Miles, and faces her people once again.

"The Day of Penance will hereby be suspended. There will be no more executions on this stage, and every criminal will have his day in front of a magistrate. Many more changes will be coming, and I thank you for your patience and support."

Cheers erupt, and "God save the queen!" rings out from the masses among the clapping. The words resound around the crowd as Starr makes her way to the back of the stage and down the steps. As she looks upon the innocent faces of the youngest boys, she hopes they never have to witness any of the horrors she's seen on that stage.

Gary peers up at her with his big brown eyes. "You missed breakfast this morning."

"I'm sorry, but I had things to do. It won't happen again." Starr pats his shoulder. "Well, it won't happen very often, I should say."

"Were you cleaning your room?" Gary asks with such innocence. "That's why Garth was late. He says it's hard to make the bed."

Gary glances at Garth's wrapped arm. He lost a lot of blood when he was shot, but the wound will heal completely.

"You dum dum. She doesn't have to do that anymore." Garth shakes his head at Gary.

He's correct, as Melinda and the maids are now here to do almost everything for her. But she still makes her own bed. It just feels right.

Starr gives Garth an appreciative nod. "I'm proud he's still cleaning his messes. I know of a little boy who needs to be better at that."

Gary's shoulders droop as his brothers laugh at him, but he tips his face up again with a smile. "I'll be better."

She doubts it. He's six, after all, but at least he's trying.

"Your Majesty, may I have a moment of your time?" Bard says, his face so serious.

"Bard." She laughs. "Can't you see we're having a very important discussion?"

"Yes, but this is official queen business." He takes her hand and tugs her towards her carriage. He tells the driver to remain there while they speak, and then he helps Starr inside, crawling behind her and closing the door.

"And what is it that's so important?" she demands playfully.

"This." Bard leans into her and wraps his arms around her waist. He brings her lips to his and smothers her with his kisses. His touch fills her with so much happiness, and she doesn't ever want to let go.

The End

Acknowledgments

Thank you to all my Beta Peeps friends for being such a supportive group: Cassie Mae, Jade Hart, Jennie Bennett, Jenny Morris, Jessica Salyer, Kelley Lynn, Lizzy Charles, Rachel Schieffelbein, and Theresa Paolo. I'm lucky to have found such a good group who is always there to offer advice and support.

Thank you also to Karen Sanders for the editing and finding so many of those stupid typos and such.

And thank you to all those who are reading my stories. You don't know how much I appreciate it.

About the Author

Reading has always been a big part of Suzi's life. She even won the most-pages-read award a few times in her junior high English class, many years ago. She started several writing projects as a kid but never actually finished anything, and then she took a big break from writing that lasted well into adulthood.

She's written in a variety of genres, including horror, suspense, and women's fiction, and has even dipped into fantasy slightly with her fairy tale retellings. She also writes young adult stories under the name Suzi Drew.

Her non-writing life includes her family and friends, her sweet and fluffy dog, and an awesome job editing fiction with some of her writer friends. (Oh wait, that's still a part of writing. Seems she can't get away from the written word!)

To find out more about Suzi,
go to SuziWieland.com

Also by Suzi Wieland

<u>Thriller Novels</u>
Black Diamond Dogs

<u>Horror Novels</u>
House of Desire

<u>Horror and Suspense Novellas/Short Stories</u>
Shallow Depths
(Un)lucky Thirteen
Long-Term Effects
The Silent Treatment
A Story to Tell
Panne Dora Pass

Twisted Twins Series
Glenda and Gus
Two for the Price of One
A Hard Split

<u>Fairy Tale Novellas</u>
The Down the Twisted Path Series
The Whole Story
An Unwanted Life
Killing Rosie
The Perfect Meal
When the Forest Cries
In the Queen's Dark Light

Please visit SuziWieland.com
for more information.

Milton Keynes UK
Ingram Content Group UK Ltd.
UKHW030951261124
451585UK00001B/40

9 798330 474547